About the Author

It is safe to say Jerry Bradley has a degree in life! He has worked in a range of jobs: building racing cars, welding, bricklaying in Europe, market trading and as a locksmith.

In 2012, his wife of 29 years became ill and he became her full time carer. This was when he discovered a passion for writing. His wife, Irene, lost her battle with Dementia in 2015.

Jerry now lives in West Sussex and is the proud Dad of two daughters, Amanda and Hannah. He does his best writing late at night and sometimes into the small hours, but still finds time for martial arts, keep fit, golf and most of all, having fun!

Please follow me on Facebook **@Jerrybradley-Author**
Website: **www.jerrybradley.co.uk**

Acknowledgements

A huge thank you to Chris Day and the amazing team at Filament. Zara, Olivia, Joan, Karen. Without your energy and professional help, this book would never have been published.

Thanks to Hannah for your help. Thanks to Richard (Stav) Watson, for your valuable contribution.

Dedication

Every book I write has to be dedicated
to my late wife Irene.

To every person, I have met in my life. I thank you all.

You have got me here. You are amazing.

I thank all my wonderful readers
and friends for your support.

SENT BACK FROM THE GRAVE
TO RIGHT A WRONG

UNFINISHED BUSINESS

IF YOU HAD THE CHANCE
TO LIVE AGAIN,
WHAT WOULD YOU DO?

JERRY BRADLEY

Author of *The Candy Man*

Published by
Filament Publishing Ltd

16, Croydon Road, Waddon, Croydon,
Surrey, CR0 4PA, United Kingdom
Telephone +44 (0)20 8688 2598
Fax +44 (0)20 7183 7186

info@filamentpublishing.com
www.filamentpublishing.com

ISBN 978-1-913192-60-0

Printed by 4edge Ltd

Contents

Unfinished Business

Prologue

Thomas Edward Stewart was sitting in the lounge of his farmhouse, a log fire blasting out heat. It was his 40th birthday. A recluse with no friends or family, he'd been on his own for 22 sad, solitary years. Staring out of the window into the darkness, he ran a finger over the scar on his face.

With memories of his parents flashing through his mind, loneliness flooded his soul. He reached for the remote to turn the TV on, anything to remove the silence. But his hands were shaking, sweat was pouring from his brow. A sudden, horrifying, intense pain clamped across his chest and down his left arm. As he keeled over, clutching his chest and fighting for breath, he knew. He was on his way to meet his maker. His final words came from instinct, from somewhere deep in his memory: "Please forgive me father, for I have..."

Tom opened his eyes. He was sitting in a dazzling white room. Astonishingly, he felt calm, an inner calmness he'd never felt before.

A woman appeared in front of him. A white flowing dress, a smile on her face, and a great big clipboard in her left hand. Her voice was soft and musical. "Hello, Tom," she said. "There's been a change of plan. I'm sending you back - you've got a job to do."

Chapter 1

A family Christmas. 25th December 2019.

The sound of a bell woke Tom. He opened his eyes and smiled as his beautiful new mother sat on his bed, a small brass bell in her hand. It was 7 am on Christmas Day.

"Morning Tom, Merry Christmas!" she said, in her warm Welsh accent. "I'm excited – our first Christmas together!" As she spoke, she pointed towards the pile of presents at the end of Tom's bed.

"Merry Christmas Mum!" said Tom. Once he'd been with Mary and Jason for a few months, their relationship had felt so natural that he'd started calling them Mum and Dad.

"Wow! Thanks so much!" he cried, staring at the pile of gifts. "I'm blown away!"

Mary's green eyes welled up. This was Tom's first Christmas with them. Her first Christmas as a mum. She wanted it to be the best ever.

She was 42 years old and five foot eight with a slim, athletic body. Mary kept herself in shape with swimming, yoga and lots of aerobic exercise. Her black hair, usually tied in a bun, wasn't yet showing grey, and her lightly-tanned skin was smooth. She was an attractive woman who turned heads wherever she went, but she'd never looked beyond her husband, Jason. Never even been tempted.

Today she was wearing a red Santa hat, red t-shirt, red skirt, red tights, and flat red shoes. Looking at her, 15-year-old Tom felt blessed. He'd been living with this amazing couple for nine months and woke every day with a smile on his face. His life before – well, that was another story, a tale he still couldn't fully understand.

For today, though, that didn't matter. Mary was smiling from ear to ear, her straight white teeth sparkling. Tom was surrounded by love and warmth, and a stack of gifts galore. Mary handed him a Christmas stocking, kissed him on his forehead and ran her fingers through his short curly blonde hair. This was Tom's second chance. He was going to grab it with both hands.

Before he could remove any of the neat wrapping on his presents, Tom's new dad entered the room, an envelope in his huge hand. A giant of a man, Jason Drake stood six foot three, weighed 15 stone and was fit as a fiddle. He was 44 years old, a good-looking sort with a lined, weathered face and grey crewcut hair.

"Merry Christmas Tom," he boomed, in a voice that matched his stature. "Here," he went on, holding out the envelope. "Before you open anything else, I think you ought to open this."

Jason smiled as Tom opened the envelope to reveal a sheath of formal-looking documents — his official adoption papers, signed, sealed and delivered. And a new surname. Thomas Edward Stewart was officially Thomas Edward Drake.

"Wow," said Tom. "Just... wow. This is the best present ever. I'm so happy. How can I ever repay you guys?"

"No need to thank us," said Mary, close to tears. "It's our pleasure. It's really our pleasure. Come on," she added, laughing. "Give your official mum a hug!"

Tom willingly obliged. Mary gently ran her fingers over the scar on his face. Jason leaned against the door frame and smiled. This was the perfect Christmas Day. The home he'd started building ten years ago was finally complete.

Sitting in a quiet, tree-lined street in Richmond, Surrey, the four-bedroom detached house had been built for love and laughter. The huge back garden, with apple trees, a handy shed, a greenhouse, and a vegetable garden as well as a flower-bordered, grassy lawn, was the perfect place for kids to play. Downstairs, a large kitchen connected to the dining room, which had sliding French doors to the back garden.

An open fire crackled on the hearth in the lounge, which led to Jason's study. At the front, a small flower bed and pea shingle driveway led to the protective hedge and six-foot fence that separated their home from the 25ft of land either side. There had only ever been one thing missing. And that day, at the children's home, he and Mary had found it. They'd found Tom.

So today would be a traditional Christmas. Decorations everywhere, a large tree twinkling with lights and tinsel in the corner of the lounge and Christmas songs in the background. They gathered around Tom's bed to exchange and open gifts.

Tom had been saving his pocket money. He got up, opened his chest of drawers and pulled out his carefully-chosen presents. Two new hairbrushes for Mary, because she was always misplacing hers, and a bottle of her favourite perfume. A set of new chisels and two woodworking saws for his dad. Even though he was the boss of over twenty employees, currently in charge of his biggest project yet — an office block in Central London he was converting into luxury apartments — he still loved to work with his hands.

Tom had new books on maths, science, and history as well as some 'impossible' Sudoku and crossword puzzle books. An extremely intelligent boy, he loved learning. But he was also a 15-year-old, so he put the books to one side for now and focused on the massive selection box and extremely fancy train set.

After all the present-opening excitement, it was time for breakfast — scrambled eggs on lightly-buttered toast. It was all they'd need, Mary had a very hearty lunch planned. Showered and dressed for the day, Tom and his dad sat and talked about history, the environment and politics. They watched TV for a while. They built up the fire in the lounge and snoozed gently in its warmth. Mary sang and smiled over her cooking. She'd insisted on doing it all by herself. She wanted Jason and Tom to spend quality time together; they so rarely had the chance because of the demands Jason's business put on him.

Lunch was amazing, the best Tom had ever had. Jason carved, Tom smiled, Mary watched with sparkling eyes as her delicious food was devoured by her two hungry boys. It was a billion years away from their previous lonely lives —Tom's and theirs. Jason and Mary had only each other until he arrived. Both their parents had passed away, and neither of them had brothers or sisters. Now, for the first time in a long time, they felt like a family.

Later, after the remains of lunch were cleared away, after the kitchen was once again spotless and they'd all enjoyed a frosty walk in the local park, after the Queen's speech and the old Christmas movies, Jason turned to Tom.

"I have one more surprise for you, my boy," he said, pulling a gift-wrapped parcel from behind his chair. Tom gasped as he opened it. A new marksman rifle with telescopic sights. A take-down model, machined with precision, that could be broken down to fit into a briefcase. Tom assembled it with ease.

His dad — his real dad — had taught him how to shoot. He'd become an expert. When Jason found out, he'd enrolled Tom in his rifle club. There was going to be a big competition the following day.

"Wow," said Tom, for what felt like the millionth time that day. "Thanks, Dad, Mum... I'm speechless. Would you believe it?" he added, laughing.

"Only the best, son," said Jason. "It's custom-made for your size and weight. We'll see how it handles tomorrow," he went on, taking the beautiful weapon from Tom's hands. "I'll lock it up in the gun cabinet for tonight."

Tom nodded, watching his dad prepare to leave the room. "Oh — wait!" he suddenly yelled, making his two parents jump. "Sorry!" he added, running upstairs two at a time. "I'll be right back!"

Tom reappeared moments later, carrying two new presents. "Surprise!" he said, handing them over. "Merry Christmas, Mum. Merry Christmas, Dad."

A gold chain and cross for Mary and a Seiko watch for Jason, who'd broken his old one at work. Tom had wanted the gifts to be a special surprise. "Thank you so much, Tom," said Mary, quietly fastening the chain around her neck. "I love it."

"Me too, Tom," said Jason. "I'll be careful with this one. It's never coming to work with me."

"I'm glad you like them," said Tom. "I wanted you both to have something special, to thank you for everything. It's been the best Christmas ever. But now," he added, yawning hugely, "It's time for bed. Goodnight guys. I love you."

"Love you too, son," said Jason, gruffly, a suspicious trace of moisture in his eye. Mary followed this son of hers, this miraculous breath of fresh air in their lives, upstairs and waited, sitting on his bed, while he showered and changed into pyjamas.

"That's me, Mum," he said, coming into the room. "Clean as a whistle."

He was so tall and handsome, this boy, thought Mary. Already the same height as her, almost 11 stone, and most of it muscle — Tom liked to train, using the old punch bag in the garage and taking long runs in the park. He was also on the school's athletic team, sprinting with near-championship times. With his curly, short blonde hair and hypnotic blue eyes, he was definitely a looker. But, as yet, there was no-one on the scene competing for his love. It was all hers, and in return she gave him a mothers' love — one like no other.

Tom jumped into bed. Mary tucked him in and kissed him on his forehead. "Night mum," he said, looking steadily up at her. "Thank you. It's been a fabulous day. I love you."

"Night Tom," said Mary, softly. I love you too." Tom shut his eyes as Mary left the room and turned out the light. He didn't feel lonely any more. The only thing missing from this incredible day had been his best friend, Sarah. He'd missed her during these holidays. They texted most days, but not today. Maybe her phone was broken. Maybe she was just too busy having a great Christmas. Tom hoped so.

He smiled at himself, at this adolescent train of thought. At his childish pleasure in having a traditional family Christmas, at owning a state-of-the-art new train set. Was this really him now? Was he really this person?

"I lived on a farm in Scotland," he thought, as he drifted slowly into sleep. *"My mum and dad died young. The farm was bankrupt. I had debts to pay. I used the only skills I had. Worked all over the world. Made a bloody fortune. Heart attack on my 40th birthday, next thing I know I'm in a waiting room with a friendly woman in a white dress telling me there's been a change of plans and I'm going back. Not into my former life, because that was complicated. Another life, a new life, a second chance. Suddenly I'm in a boy's body, but I'm still me, right down to the scar on my face. I woke up on a London street, with a kindly woman from*

the Salvation Army leaning over me, offering shelter and food. Someone arrived and took me to a children's home. I kept my story secret – who'd believe me? They'd lock me up. I pleaded amnesia. I had no family, there were no records. There was no way anyone could find out the truth. Christ, I hardly believe it myself. But this is it. I'm going to make it work. I'm going to be the best I can be. I'm going to find this job I have to do, and do it. I'm going to take this second chance."

Tom fell asleep and dreamed of trains.

Chapter 2

26th December. Boxing Day.

The alarm sounded. Tom glanced out of the window. No point thinking about going on his daily 5-mile run, it was snowing again. He put on boxing gear instead and went out to the garage, turned on the lights and slid on his bag gloves. The heavy-duty 6ft punch bag was old and belonged to Jason, who used it to de-stress after a hard day at work.

After a 45-minute cardio workout, Tom was drenched in sweat and feeling good. A quick shower, dried and dressed. He cleaned his en suite bathroom and tidied his room. Both were spotless. With no school work to do, he sat at his desk and focused on a crossword puzzle until Mary's voice floated up from the bottom of the stairs: "Breakfast will be ready in ten minutes!"

"Thanks, mum!" he called back, then finished his crossword, washed his hands and zoomed downstairs. Jason was drinking coffee and Mary was rustling up a full English. A great start to the day. Over breakfast, they chatted about the competition, the blue ribbon championship. Although he was the youngest member of the club, Tom was a great shot and stood a good chance of winning. "Remember to relax and breathe slowly," Jason was saying, always the coach. "Give it your best shot Tom. That's all you can do."

"You know me, Dad," said Tom, smiling and rolling his eyes. "That's my plan!"

Mary didn't like rifles or guns and never went to the club. It wasn't her thing, but she'd be cheering on her boy from the house. She gave Tom a hug and wished him luck. Jason kissed his wonderful wife and opened the front door. It was time to focus on the day ahead.

"Ready, Tom?" he said picking up the rifle case.

"Born ready, Dad," Tom replied.

Built inside a disused railway tunnel, Feltham Rifle Club was a seven-mile drive from their home. On the way there, Tom turned on his phone to check for a text from Sarah. Nothing. He'd try to catch her later that day, once the competition was over.

They arrived at the club. Inside, the place was buzzing. Assisted by Jason, Tom adjusted and loaded his new rifle. He had time to practice before the competition began.

Even through his ear defenders, he could hear a lot of noise from the adjacent cubicle. It was Sarah's adoptive father, George Miller, along with his entourage. A very ambitious politician, George had come from a working-class background to reach Deputy Prime Minister in record time. Everyone knew he had plans to get right to the top. He'd spent years making friends with powerful and wealthy people, who he hoped would help him get to where he wanted to be. What he wasn't was a marksman. In fact, Tom thought, watching him fumble his way around his rifle, he was probably the worst marksman on the planet.

It was time to select competition slots. Numbers were drawn from a hat to see who'd shoot first. Tom. George Miller stepped out to watch with the utmost interest. He'd seen Tom shoot before, but not in a competition. Not under pressure.

Tom loaded the rifle, breathing deeply, mentally running through the competition procedure. Six shots. The first target at 100m, then each successive one would be 50m further away. Just a matter of taking his time and acing each one. Lowering his rifle for the first shot, he took a deep, calm breath, aimed and fired. Bullseye. Ten points. Five shots later, Tom had six bullseyes, each shot dead centre of its target. Maximum points. George Miller nodded to himself, impressed. Jason clapped his son's back, unable to speak. The boy never seemed daunted by anything. Nerves of steel.

Two hours later, to rapturous applause, Tom held a large trophy in his hands, Jason smiling and laughing beside him. George Miller sidled over to shake hands. "Hello, Jason," he said, with his best fake politician smile. "I can't believe a kid won the club championship! The boy did you proud."

"George," Jason replied, nodding. He wasn't a fan of George Miller, seeing him for what he was — a slimy, bullshitting politician. But he was also a member of Jason's rifle club, so he felt he should make polite conversation. "I'm very proud of Tom," he added. "And not just for his shooting skills."

Tom stayed quiet and gripped his trophy tighter, in case George tried to steal it.

Exchanged niceties for a couple of wasted minutes. Jason had only one thought, what did George want?

On the pleasant drive home, Jason wondered again what Miller wanted. He'd noticed him keeping a beady eye on Tom, and knew he had to want something — he never normally bothered himself to speak to Jason. But who cared? Look what his son had just done. "Tom, I'm so bloody proud of you," he said. "You showed them all today. You raised the bar, son, to a whole new level."

Tom looked up from his phone to smile at his dad. Still no word from Sarah.

Mary was waiting by the window for their return, excited by the news of Tom's win. Back inside the warm lounge, Jason opened a bottle of Champagne and poured three glasses. He handed a half-full glass to Tom and one to Mary. Tom sipped the sparkling liquid and smiled.

"Congratulations, young man!" Jason roared with delight. "I've never seen anyone shoot that well in a competition. It was incredible."

Tom picked up the trophy and handed it to Mary. "I won the competition for you" he said. "For both of you. To say thanks for — well, for everything."

The afternoon shot by. Finally, after supper, it was time. Tom had been waiting all day for this moment. Dragging out the huge new train set, he and Jason cleared the dining room table and set it up. Track, buildings, bridges, scenery, tiny people — it was all superb. Within a couple of hours, a miniature Mallard Pullman was whizzing around the track, followed by its parlour and brake cars, filled (in Tom's imagination) with little 1920s characters enjoying the scenery as it zoomed by.

At 9pm, as they were shutting everything down for the night, Tom pointed to the window. "Mum, Dad, look!" he said. "It's snowing again. Giant snowman tomorrow!" Grinning, he made his way upstairs, followed by Mary who, despite his teenage years, liked to tuck him in at night.

Washed and in pyjamas, Tom jumped into bed and accepted his mum's hug. "Are you happy Tom?" she asked. "You know... really happy? With us?"

"One hundred percent, mum," said Tom. "I'm so lucky..." He paused, unsure if he should go further. He didn't want to trouble his parents, but they said it was always best to be honest. Mary watched in some concern as he bit his lower lip and looked up at her. "Mum... can I ask a question?" he said.

"Of course, son," she replied, trying not to look terrified.

"It's... it's just school," he said. "I'm not sure about it. I don't seem to fit in. They call me names, push me around and stuff. No-one wants to talk to me and I don't know why. It's like — like I'm invisible or something..."

"Oh, Tom," said Mary, hugging her son again. "I'm so sorry. Kids can be so awful. I just don't get it. You're bright, you're funny, you're athletic, you do great in class..." Mary paused, gaining a brief insight into why the other kids perhaps didn't love her boy. She decided not to share.

"Listen, son," she said. "You're special. Your dad and I, we couldn't be prouder of you. I think those other kids are jealous, to be honest. But I'm sorry for it. I wish you had just one special friend."

"Oh, I do!" cried Tom. "Sarah Miller! She's brilliant. She sits next to me in class, we spend all our breaks together. She's my best friend. She's not bothered about the scar on my face."

Mary smiled sadly. It bothered her that Tom never had friends around or was invited anywhere. She gently touched his face. All that money to put Tom in a top school, to give him the very best education money could buy. She sighed. Why did kids have to be so bloody horrible?

"I'm sorry Mum," said Tom. "I didn't want to make you sad. It's just that it makes me angry, and I don't want to be angry. It's such a negative emotion. I just want to learn."

"I wish I knew how to help," said Mary. "I could have a word with the headmaster when term starts again?"

"No mum, don't say anything," said Tom. "It'll only make things worse. I just – I just wanted to let you know, to chat it through," he added. "I wanted to be honest, like you always say. It's okay – I'll keep my head down and get on with it, it'll be okay. I can deal with it. But I hate it when they start on Sarah."

"Tell you what, Tom," said Mary, "Why don't you ask her to come over tomorrow. She can help you with that snowman, stay for dinner, spend the whole day if she wants to. What do you think?"

"Brilliant!" said Tom, immediately lifting his phone from the bedside table, face all smiles. He sent a text to Sarah, hoping for a fast reply. Mary ran her fingers through his hair, hoping his friend would agree. She wanted everything for this boy. She'd never thought in a million years she could love someone this much. Her heart had almost burst when she'd first set eyes on him at the children's home. They'd had to go through a long, frustrating adoption process, but it had been worthwhile. She loved him. His blue eyes, his smile. His warmth and innocence, his charm and humour. Suddenly his face lit up with the light of his phone. A text from Sarah: *Yes, please, I'd love to see you, can't wait, excited.*

Mary watched her son, engrossed in his reply: *Great! See you tomorrow. I've got you a present. Sorry I couldn't give it to you before school broke up, had to wait til dad took me shopping. Mum's going to call your mum to arrange a time.*

Sarah answered almost immediately: *Wow, thanks! I have something for you, too, see you tomorrow, night! x*

"Sarah would love to come over," said Tom. "That's great," said Mary, smiling at this high-speed exchange, so unlike the way she'd talked to her pals as a child. "And Tom? Don't worry about those kids at school. Just wait until you get older and the other kids understand you more. All the boys will want to be your friend — and all the girls will be chasing you. You'll have to run like the wind!"

"I like the sound of that," said Tom, snuggling down. "Thanks for the chat mum. You're brilliant."

Mary turned away, wiping her tears, then kissed his forehead. "I'll phone Sarah's mum now," she said, "Invite her and George over for a coffee and a nice chat."

"Thanks, mum, you're the best," answered Tom. "But can you come back after you've done that? I have a surprise for you."

"Of course I will," said Mary, heading downstairs.

Three miles away, in her freezing farmhouse bedroom, a very excited Sarah Miller was punching the air.

"Yes!" she hissed, to herself. "Oh, I love you, Tom,". Pulling out a huge diary, Sarah grabbed her favourite pen in her cold hand and started to write.

Dear Tom. I've missed you so much it hurts. I'm sorry I didn't text you yesterday, I was just too upset. I can't take much more of living here. I'm so sad and lonely. I feel like I'm drowning. I would have run away if I hadn't met you. I hate the holidays and not seeing you at school. I can't wait until tomorrow. Oh, please rescue me. Please.

I haven't told you everything about George. If I did, I think you might punch him. When he's drunk, his face goes red, he gets angry and rants and rants at me. He forgets I'm deaf. I spend most of my time in my bedroom, trying to stay away from him. Lisa is scared of him too. I've tried and tried to get her to see sense and leave him, but she's frightened. It's so sad. She could have a good life away from him. I hate him for what he's done to both of us.

There is so much more I want to say to you, but I have to stop writing, my hands are freezing. I love you.

Closing the book, Sarah tucked her hands under the two duvets. She shut her eyes and tried to sleep, tried to dream of Tom coming to the rescue.

Back at the Drake house, Mary reappeared in Tom's bedroom. "It's all arranged," she said. "George and Lisa will drop Sarah off at about 11. Sorry I took so long, Lisa wouldn't stop talking, she was so pleased to hear from me."

"Thanks, mum," said Tom, "Here. An extra present Dad and I got for you. He says you need them."

Mary opened the present and laughed. It was a pair of thick bed socks.

"Dad says he loves you to bits, but you've got cold feet and you try to warm your feet on him," grinned her son. "So the problem's solved. We love you, mum!"

"I'll give you dad cold feet," said Mary, still laughing. "The cheek!" Mary hugged Tom, squeezing him tight.

"Night mum. Thanks for a wonderful day," yawned Tom. "I love you."

"Night Tom," said Mary. "Love you too. Sleep well, and thanks for the bed socks." Pausing in the doorway to turn out the light, she added: "They'll come in handy to strangle your dad."

Chapter 3

Mary shut the door and went downstairs for a chat with Jason. Pouring a whisky for him and a medicinal brandy for herself, she sat down beside him.

"I believe that boy has quite a crush on Sarah Miller," she said. "Oh, and thank you for my bed socks. They'll keep me warm tonight, while you sleep in the spare room."

"Cold feet, warm heart," responded Jason, grinning. "You know we love you just the way you are."

"I forgive you," replied his wife. "And I forgot to thank you yesterday for giving Tom extra money to buy the chain and cross. It's beautiful."

"Don't thank me," said Jason. "Tom bought it himself. He must have saved every penny of his pocket money since he's been with us. I helped him chose gifts for Sarah, as well. He's spent nothing on himself. He earns his pocket money, then spends it on gifts for us."

"That boy is the best gift we could ever wish for," said Mary, settling into the couch beside him. "By the way, Lisa and George Miller are bringing Sarah over tomorrow. Let's make sure they have a wonderful day."

"Don't smother them, Mary," said Jason. "Let them do whatever they want. We'll stay in the shadows. Let them have fun."

"Okay, bossy boots, you're a wise man. That's why I love you so much." Mary hesitated a moment before bringing up what was most on her mind. Jason was a big, powerful man. If he knew his son was being pushed around... But no point lying or pretending about it. "Did you know Tom is being bullied at school?" she said. "He told me just now." Stealing a look at her husband, Mary was surprised to see him smiling to himself.

"I don't think we need to worry too much," he said. "Have you seen him working out on the old punch bag? That boy has raw talent, he's as hard as nails. He's smart enough — if he decides to stop the bullying, I'll back him."

"I'm allowed to worry," pretend-pouted Mary. "That's what mums do. But you're a good man, Jason Drake, and you're right. We'll help Tom to blossom in his own time and his own way."

"I believe Tom's helping us, too," answered Jason. "We've never been happier — it's like the three musketeers. The last few months have been amazing." He raised his glass. "Here's to a bright future," he said. "Here's to Thomas Drake. Our boy Tom."

"Our boy Tom," echoed Mary.

They sat in silence and watched the snowflakes falling. Mary broke it. "Do you think Tom needs more therapy?" she said. "He still has occasional nightmares. I can't even think about what he went through on the streets. And no one knows about the life he had before that. Imagine if the woman from the Salvation Army hadn't found him."

"I don't know Mary, he seems genuinely happy and I think he's doing okay," said Jason. "Look at his school reports — he's a genius, and that's a fact. And he can talk to us about anything, he knows that. But I'm not an expert. Look, I'll have a chat with him tomorrow, ask him if he thinks he needs more therapy. He's sensible enough and old enough to make that decision himself."

"You're right again, Jason," said Mary, leaning her head on his shoulder. He put his strong arm around her, and they settled down, wrapped in warmth and the glow from the TV screen.

Tom watched the snowflakes falling from his bedroom window. He hoped it wouldn't stop Sarah from coming over tomorrow. Would the roads be passable? He hadn't seen any grit lorries. Sarah lived 3 miles away, on a farm with 40 acres of land. He hoped she wouldn't be snowed in.

He got the bible he'd been given by the Salvation Army out of his school bag, and put it under his pillow. He wasn't overly religious, having a vague sense of belief in something indefinable but benevolent. Kneeling by his bed, he said a short prayer for Sarah before jumping back under the covers. Somehow, if his prayers could be answered, he'd make Sarah's life better. Sooner, rather than later. He was worried about her. He knew life on the farm was crappy. He knew she was lonely and sad. He knew he was the only person on the planet she trusted.

Chapter 4

27th December.

The alarm woke Tom at 6 am. He was eager, thrilled and nervous about Sarah's visit. He quickly made a list of things to do and planned out his day. First: tidy his bedroom. Since it was already mostly spotless, it didn't take long to tick that off his list.

Jason and Mary were enjoying a much-needed lie-in, so Tom headed down to the kitchen and drew the blinds. There was lots of snow. Snowman! But would Sarah want to build a snowman? Was it too childish? He'd never built one. In his previous life, on his dad's sheep farm, snow was a killer, not a plaything. From the age of eight, if he saw snow, it meant searching and shovels and desperate efforts to save the sheep, especially if it was late in the winter and the lambs had started arriving.

But no. He needed to forget his past. This was a new life, new territory – a friend coming over. He'd never had a friend visit before. His hands shook a little bit as he set up the coffee machine, sliced bread for toast, hunted out the egg poacher. What if Sarah thought he was a kid? Or a geek?

Would she laugh at him for having a train set? What if she thought he was a big baby? He started to feel panicky, not like himself at all.

"I need to get a grip," he mumbled to himself.

"Morning Tom," came his mother's voice, behind him. "Who were you talking to? Mr Nobody?"

"Morning mum," he replied, hoping she hadn't noticed his little jump of surprise. "I - I'm making breakfast. Sorry, bit on edge. Not sure what to wear today. Don't know if the snowman is a good idea. Do you think it's a good idea? Should I leave the train set out or put it away? Shall we make lunch now so it's ready for later? I need to clear the snow and ice off the steps. Do you think the roads will be OK?" He stopped, realising he was babbling, laughing at himself and the look on Mary's face. "I'm way out of my comfort zone here, mum," he said. "In case you couldn't tell. I'm really nervous. Sarah's just so awesome."

The innocence of youth, thought Mary, ruffling Tom's curly hair. She remembered her first date with Jason, literally falling head over heels when her ridiculously high shoes had caught in the restaurant carpet and she'd tripped right into his arms. It was the first time in her life she'd felt safe and loved.

"Let's start by having breakfast, then you can have a chat with your dad," she said. "Just try to relax. Be yourself. Have fun today."

"Thanks, mum," said Tom, drawing a long breath. "I feel better already."

After a family breakfast, Mary went upstairs to sort out Tom's clothes for the day, leaving him and Jason to have a manly chat. "I've been thinking about showing you some of my boxing moves," said Jason. "My dad taught me to box. We could even train together, if you like. I used to be in a boxing club, and I fought as an amateur in my teens."

"Wow, Dad," said Tom, genuinely impressed. "That would be brilliant." Looking sidelong at his father, he added: "Did mum have a word with you about school?"

"Yes Tom, she did. I told her I'm pretty sure you can handle yourself. I've watched you work out on the old punch bag. To be honest, you could probably teach me how to box."

"Well, how about we teach each other?" said Tom, smiling up at him. "Look, Dad, I don't want you or mum to worry. I want you to be happy. As happy as you've made me."

"Ah, all good parents worry," said Jason. "It's our job. But listen, son, do you think it would help you to have more therapy? I know you're still having nightmares, and your mum said you're worried about getting angry at school."

"I think I'm okay, thanks Dad," answered Tom. "Honestly, I've never been happier. I haven't had a bad nightmare for months, and school's alright, really. I can deal with it. Mum says in a couple of years everyone will want to be my friend and the girls will be chasing me. So there's that to look forward to."

"Alright Tom," said Jason, laughing in spite of himself. "I'm glad we had this chat though. And if you change your mind — well, you know you can talk to me about anything."

"Actually, Dad, there are a couple of things I want to ask," said Tom.

"Anything, son."

"Do girls like train sets? And building snowmen?"

An hour or so later, Tom's phone beeped. Sarah. *I'm so excited about today, can't wait to see you. I'm also nervous. I hope your parents like me. xxx*

Tom showed the text to his dad. "What'll I say?" he said. "I don't want to say anything that'll mess today up." Jason smiled, put his right hand on his heart and looked at Tom. "Just reply from your heart, son," he said. "That's always worked for me."

Nodding, Tom typed: *I'm excited, can't wait until you arrive. My mum and dad will love you. Do you want to build a snowman? And do you like train sets?*

You have a train set? I'm your girl! And I'd love to build a snowman. See you soon! 😊 *x*

Jason shook his head and smiled as he watched his son typing his messages. He'd never seen him this excited. He poured himself another coffee, nearly choked on it when Tom punched the air, shouting "YES!! Oh, sorry, Dad. It's just – Sarah likes train sets. And she's really up for building a snowman with me. Would you believe it?"

Jason put his giant hands on Tom's shoulders. "One piece of advice young man," he said, impressively. "Never try to impress anyone. Just be yourself. People will love you for who you are. Now, I'll clear the steps, and you go up and get dressed. It'll be interesting to see George again," he added. "I'm sure he wants something from us. It's just a hunch — maybe it's just because I don't trust politicians."

"What shall I talk to Sarah about today?" said Tom, who was barely listening. "We mostly talk about school."

"Oh, I don't know," said Jason. "Normal stuff. Her life, her hopes, what she wants to do when school's over, what kind of music she likes. Just relax son – I'm sure today will be fun."

"Okay dad," said Tom, musing all this over. "Thanks for the chat."

Outside with his snow shovel and bag of salt, Jason cleared the snow from the front steps, allowing his mind to turn over some of his own worries. His latest project was massive. He'd bought an old office block overlooking the Thames, close to the London Eye, and was flat out converting it into luxury apartments. The penthouse was near completion, but the bank manager had been on his back, giving him a hard time. He'd been having chest pains, which he told himself were being caused by stress. It wasn't a situation he was used to. Six months behind schedule, with outstanding invoices to pay and continual barriers to progress being thrown at him by the council's building and planning people. It seemed to be a constant battle. If he'd been a paranoid man, he'd have thought someone was actively working against him, trying to stop him succeeding. Money was tight and getting tighter. Taking his boots off and laying his tools aside in the garage, he stepped back into the warmth of his family home.

"That boy is in overdrive," said Mary, coming up behind him and wrapping him in a hug. "It's so cute. He wants everything perfect for Sarah. Are you okay?" she asked, as he turned round to return her embrace. "You look tired. Jason, you know you can talk to me. I'm here, we're a team."

"I'm okay thanks," he said, smiling at her. "Just the usual business ups and downs. I had a chat with Tom," he went on quickly, seeing her begin to frown. "I really think he's okay, you know. Says he doesn't want more therapy, but he'll tell us if anything changes. That's good, right?" Mary smiled and kissed her husband.

Twenty minutes later, Tom came running down the stairs and into the kitchen. "Do I look okay?" he panted. "I'm going for the casual look, is that alright?" He wore blue jeans, red Santa socks, a red t-shirt, and his favourite red hoodie. Mary nodded her approval. "You look handsome Tom," she said. "Cool and casual. Just right."

"Thanks, mum," said her son, beaming at her and dashing off again. "I'm going to set out the chessboard!" he shouted back at them. "Sarah plays; I'll give her a game later!"

"Sometimes I wonder if that lad is 15 going on 30," said Jason, shaking his head. "I hope Sarah Miller appreciates all the effort he's making."

"I'm sure she will," Mary replied and did a twirl in her favourite red dress. "How do I look?"

"Stunning," said Jason, adding quickly: "As usual."

"How well do you know George?" Mary asked, grinning at him. "He's high up in the government, isn't he? Lisa did tell me ages ago, but I can't remember. You know I'm not interested in politics and never will be. They all lie so much."

"He's Deputy PM, love, there's only one level higher he could go!" chuckled Jason. "I don't know him that well, though. I only see him at the rifle club, and he hardly ever deigns to speak to me. He is, without a doubt, one of the worst marksmen I've ever seen. And I'll be honest, politician or otherwise, I don't think I'd like or trust him one bit."

"I used to meet Lisa at the leisure centre for coffee and a chat after yoga," said Mary. "She hardly ever spoke about George, mostly about Sarah. I like Lisa. Actually, I really miss those chats. I haven't seen her for ages."

"Maybe it's time we started going out again," said Jason. "See old friends and make some new ones. We never go out as a couple anymore. I'm sure Tom would be fine by himself for a few hours, and that he wouldn't mind."

"Sounds like a good idea," Mary replied. "I mean, nothing crazy or anything. Maybe once a month?"

"Done," said Jason. "Give me a kiss to seal the deal."

At 11am on the dot, there was the sound of tyres crunching up the driveway. "Let's give the Millers a warm welcome," said Jason. "Watch out!" he added, "Here comes Tom!" Sure enough, Tom was bouncing down the stairs at a rapid rate, shouting: "The Millers are here! The Millers are here!" Zooming past them, he took a deep breath and stood on guard at the front door.

He watched the Millers get out of their new, government-issue Jaguar. It was black and stood out in sharp contrast with the white, snow-covered driveway. Tom opened the door as they reached it, and Sarah ran up the steps and embraced him, before stepping back, slightly embarrassed. "Hi Sarah," said Tom, repeating the phrase in sign language. He'd learned it in his previous life — his birth mother had been deaf. "It's so good to see you!"

"I'm so happy to be here," said Sarah, using the same speak-and-sign method as Tom. Her voice had that characteristic muted quality of the deaf, and Tom loved it. It felt like her words were wrapped in the thickest, warmest blanket and it made him feel good to hear her. "We're glad to have you," he answered, proudly gesturing her inside.

Sarah smiled and stepped in, followed by George and Lisa. Tom shut the door as Jason and Mary greeted their guests. "Hello Mrs. Miller, Deputy Prime Minister," he said, shaking each by the hand. Jason and Mary suppressed their smiles, watching this frantic boy play the perfect gentleman. Mary made a mental note to ask where he'd learned sign language.

Coats and shoes off, everyone went into the lounge for coffee. Tom passed bowls of snacks and plates of biscuits, smiling delightedly at his friend the whole time. Jason watched George, whose sharp little eyes were fixated on Tom.

Chapter 5

"Come on Sarah, let's give the adults some space," said Tom. "Would you like a glass of milk? Juice? A hot chocolate?"

"Actually, I'd like to give you your present first," Sarah replied. "If that's okay with you?"

"Cool! Let's go up to my room," said Tom, leading the way.

Upstairs, enjoying the warmth of Tom's room, Sarah handed him his gift. "I hope you like it," she said, shyly. "I saved up for ages. Merry late Christmas."

Tom opened the bright wrapping to reveal the hardback book about legendary Olympic sprinters he'd been wanting for ages. "Wow!" he gasped. "I love it, Sarah. Thank you so much! Here, these are for you." He handed her a soft parcel, wrapped in snow-white tissue with a gold bow. "I hope you like them," he said, as she carefully untied the wrapping. "They'll keep you warm."

Sarah watched as bright red folds of the softest woollen scarf fell from the packaging, along with matching gloves and an adorable knitted beret. "Oh, Tom," she said, wrapping the scarf around her shoulders. "These are exactly what I need. Our house is so cold!"

She looked up at him, but he was already holding out a second parcel, as beautifully-wrapped as the first. This time, she ripped the paper off and opened the red velvet box inside. A gold chain glinted from a bed of white satin. Overwhelmed, she dropped the box on her lap.

"Oh Tom!" she said, throwing her arms round him. "I love it! Thank you so much, it's the best present ever. Can you help me put it on, please? I've never had jewellery before."

Sarah moved her scarf and hair out of the way. Tom, holding the chain, gently put his arms over her head and fastened it at the back of her neck. "There you go," he said, turning her to face him. "I'm so glad you like it."

She burst into tears. He looked at her for a second, horror-struck, then dived for the box of tissues on his desk and handed her one. "Don't cry!"

he begged. "Please, don't cry! I'm sorry, I didn't mean to make you sad, I only want you to be happy, you're my best friend and I—"

"You DO make me happy," choked out Sarah, laughing and sobbing at the same time. "More than you'll ever know! Oh, I've missed you so much!"

She wrapped her arms around him, again, sniffling into his red hoodie. He held her tight.

Downstairs, George was chatting with Jason. "How did Tom learn to shoot so well?" he said. "The boy's got talent."

"Tom's a natural marksman," Jason replied, faking a smile. "I quite agree with you, he's a talented young man."

Sitting with Lisa, Mary was having a much pleasanter time, although she had a feeling Lisa wasn't her usual self. She looked sad, despite the flawless makeup and stretched-out smile.

"It's so good to see you again Lisa," she said. "I'm so glad Sarah and Tom are friends."

"Sarah never stops talking about him," Lisa replied. "He's helped her so much. She doesn't have many friends, but she's an intelligent girl and never lets her disability hold her back."

"She's beautiful," said Mary. "She's always welcome here — and so are you. So don't be a stranger, okay?"

"I've never seen Sarah so happy," said Lisa, smiling. "The best thing I ever did was get her into that school. And now she has Tom by her side. I'm so very grateful."

Jason did the rounds, refilling the coffee cups. He was happy they were all getting on, for Tom's sake, even if he could have lived without George and his nonsense about the new dawn of politics, and Making Britain Great Again. Jason knew bullshit when he heard it, and he'd already heard enough of this rubbish from the other side of the Atlantic.

Upstairs, Sarah had stemmed her tears. She let go of Tom's neck and sat back. "I love you," she signed.

"I love you too," Tom replied. They both blushed crimson, grinning.

"The chain is beautiful, Tom," Sarah went on. "I'm sorry I cried. It's just so amazing to be here. I've missed you."

"I've missed you too," said Tom. "And thank you for my present. It's brilliant."

They looked at each other and smiled. Tom wished he could tell her the truth. But she'd just think he was crazy. He had no choice but to keep his secret locked away.

"Tell you what," he said. "How about that hot drink? I make the best hot chocolate. Then we'll go and make that snowman."

"Yes, please," signed Sarah. "But — can I kiss you first?"

Feeling his heart flip over, Tom nodded. She smiled, and leaned forward, and delivered the tiniest, slightest peck on the lips. It was over in a second. It felt longer.

Hand in hand, they walked downstairs, where George and Lisa were putting their coats on. George nodded at Tom. "Right, young lady," said Lisa, brightly. "Enjoy your day. I hope you have lots of fun."

"We'll drop Sarah home about eight," said Jason. "If that's okay with you?"

"Yes, that's perfect," said Lisa, stepping out of the door as George crunched his way back to the car. Tom's eyes burned into his back.

Three hours later, a gigantic snowman had taken possession of the back green, complete with a hat sprinkled in bird seed. Sarah's beautiful long, straight blond hair was coming loose from its tidy ponytail, her cheeks were glowing pink and her blue eyes sparkled and shone. At 5ft 4 she was slight in build, maybe a little underfed, and, like Tom, she was athletic and one of the top sprinters in the school. Mary thought she could use a little feeding up. So could her mother, she reflected.

Jason was in his study, wondering why George Miller was so interested in his son. The way George stared at Tom made him uneasy. What did the man want? Jason trusted his instincts, they were usually spot on. Sighing, he shut his laptop. He wasn't going to figure that out today. The business was in trouble, no denying it, but right now his mind was elsewhere. On his family.

Jason had built his business, one step at a time, from small house extensions, patios, garden walls, renovating properties, investing in land and building new homes. Mary had been with him most of the way and worked as hard as him. They'd built a successful business together. The saying that behind every successful man stands a woman wasn't true in their case. They stood together. Mary had only recently taken a step away to be a proud, full-time mum. Jason knew that at some point he would have to speak to her about the business. He was dreading that conversation.

Mary was sitting on a stool, watching the kids from the kitchen window when he went through. "Looks like they're having fun," he said. "Want a coffee?"

"Yes, please," she said, still looking out the window. "I hope they don't get too cold. It's freezing outside."

"Mary, please stop worrying," said Jason, coming over to give her a hug. "You'll get wrinkles," he added, giving her a playful kiss on her smooth cheek.

Tom came zooming inside. "Hi Dad! Can you take a photo of us by the snowman? It looks brilliant!" he said. "Of course, son," Jason replied, letting Mary go and patting his pockets for his phone. "Great job — it really is fantastic!"

Mary smiled as they all trooped outside. This was the closest to being a child she'd ever seen Tom. It made her happy.

Tom and Sarah stood on each side of the snowman as Jason took photos, then bombarded him with snowballs they'd stashed behind it.

They all came roaring back into the kitchen, shrugging wet coats, hats, gloves, and shoes off before charging into the lounge, where they flopped down in front of the fire. Side by side, happy and warm, no words needed.

When they were thoroughly warmed, Mary heated some hearty home-made soup and served it with crusty bread, straight from the oven. They all sat around the kitchen table, laughing and joking, Sarah lip-reading Mary and Jason, Tom staring at her in rapt admiration. She and Tom cleared up and made coffee afterwards.

"Thank you, Mrs Drake, for a lovely lunch," she said, handing over Mary's coffee. "And thank you for having me here."

"It's a pleasure," said Mary, smiling at her son's beautiful little friend.

The rest of the afternoon was spent in a pleasant haze of activities — an imaginary trip to the seaside, with the gorgeous sleek blue curves of the Mallard leading the way. Four games of chess, which resulted in a tie – two games apiece. A couple of crossword puzzles and a browse through Tom's new book. "It's so much fun, being here," said Sarah, with just the slightest of sighs. She turned to Mary and Jason, who were snuggled up on the sofa. "Mr. and Mrs Drake, this is the best day of my life," she said, seriously. "Thank you."

"We're so happy you're here," said Mary, trying not to get misty-eyed at the earnest little face in front of her. "And please call me Mary, darling. This gentle giant next to me is Jason."

"Okay — Mary," said Sarah, blushing. "Thank you."

Chapter 6

The day seemed to fly by. Too soon for Tom, it was 6pm, less than two hours left with Sarah. He glanced at his watch, wondering how he could stop time. After a deliciously warming casserole cooked by Mary, watched through the kitchen window by a smiling snowman, they gathered in the lounge to watch a movie. While Jason ferreted among the DVD collection with Sarah, Tom looked out of the bay window. It was still snowing; a picture-postcard blanket of white snow lay all around. Suddenly he grinned.

"Mum," he said, "It's been snowing all afternoon. The roads'll be dangerous — maybe it would be best if Sarah stays the night?"

Mary smiled. Jason's 4x4 had traction control and was fitted with snow chains. But she knew he didn't want Sarah to leave, so she nodded "Good idea," she said. "Ask Sarah if she wants to stay, then I'll contact Lisa and make sure she's happy with the arrangement."

"Yes please Mary," chipped in Sarah, who'd been watching the conversation. "I'm sure Lisa and George won't mind. I'd much rather be here — you have a beautiful home. And it's so warm!" She snapped her mouth shut, worried she was giving away too much. But Mary wisely didn't comment, and simply sent a text to Lisa. The reply came back quickly, giving permission for Sarah to stay.

After their movie it was time to get ready for bed. Tom showed Sarah to the guest room. Mary, as always, had been busy. She'd already made up the bed and got extra blankets to make sure Sarah could be as warm as she liked. Tom gave Sarah a set of pyjamas, a toothbrush, and a large, fluffy towel, then went back to his room while she changed.

Mary came in and smiled at her son. "Are you okay?" she asked. "Does Sarah have everything she needs?" "Yes, thanks mum," Tom replied. "I'm going to get her settled, then I'll head for bed myself. Thanks for a fantastic day," he added. "It was even better than I hoped."

Ten minutes later, Sarah was ready and snuggling down in her bed. Tom smiled from the doorway. "Light on or off?" he signed. "Off, please," said Sarah. "It's been a fantastic day, Tom. I feel like a princess." He kissed her cheek, switched off the light and gently closed the bedroom door behind him. Sarah was a princess, and he was going to rescue her. He was going to give it his best shot.

He walked downstairs, to say goodnight to his mum and dad, who he could hear having a conversation. As he got to the lounge door, he stopped. Jason's words seemed to glue his feet to the floor.

"It's not as bad as it could be," he was saying. "I'm sorry to burden you with it, but I had to let you know love. It's only fair. We're in a deep hole, I won't lie. But if we can just ride it out long enough to sell the penthouse, things will get back on track." He sighed. "It's been a bastard year, love, I can tell you. Sorry."

"Oh Jason, no wonder you're stressed out," said Mary. "But look, whatever happens, we still have each other, and our boy Tom. I'd live in a wet cardboard box with you both — although I know it won't come to that," she added quickly, and it sounded like she was trying to smile. "I'm just saying," she went on, "For better, for worse. Remember?"

"I'm a lucky man," said Jason. "I love you, Mary."

"I love you too," said Mary, and there was the soft sound of a kiss. Tom took a deep breath, and smiled as he opened the door. "Sarah's all tucked up in bed," he said, cheerfully. "She's had a brilliant day. What do you think of her?"

"We adore her!" said Mary, smiling at him from Jason's arms. "We're glad you both had a good day."

Tom gave his dad a big hug. "Goodnight dad," he said. "Thanks for everything today."

"Night, Tom."

Mary raced Tom up the stairs, tucked him in and kissed him on his forehead. "'Night, Tom," she whispered "Love you."

"'Night mum. I love you too."

Sarah, switching her bedside lamp on, pulled her diary from her bag.

Dear Tom, she wrote. *Thank you so much for a wonderful day. It's been the happiest of my life, so much fun. Mary and Jason are amazing. I had a hot shower for the first time in weeks. I feel warm, safe and loved. I was so empty, so sad and lonely before you came into my life. You've changed everything. I'll do anything to keep that beautiful smile on your face, and make you the happiest man on earth. That I promise. We'll be married in a church, have two beautiful children, one girl, one boy, and we'll look after them and love them. Jason and Mary will be amazing grandparents. We'll name our daughter Alice, like Alice in Wonderland, and name our son Thomas, after you. My mum would have loved you. I wish you could have met her, but life before you was harsh. I had a sister. She lost her battle with drugs, and died. My dad couldn't forgive himself, and committed suicide. My mum had a heart attack shortly afterwards. Life was terrible. But now I'm with you, it's amazing. Apart from George. He ruined Christmas Day. Lisa did try to make it special, but he drank too much and got red and angry and frightened both of us so much we ended up locked in my bedroom until he went to sleep. Never mind, Tom. That's gone. I'm just going to think about you. My chain is so beautiful — I'll wear it until the day I die. I'm so lucky. I know you'll do anything to make me happy and keep me safe. You're the love of my life, my perfect match. We'll have a fantastic life together, just you wait and see, my Tom. I love you, and always will.*

Closing the diary, Sarah picked up her phone. In the other room, Tom's phone beeped. A text from Sarah.

It's been a fab day, thank you so much. I love you. xxx

I love you too. I thought you'd be asleep by now.

Are you lonely?

I'm okay, are you lonely?

Yes.

I'll come and sit by your side until you fall asleep.

Really?

Yes. I'm going to keep you safe. For as long as I live. That's a promise.

I feel safe when I'm with you.

I'm on my way.

Tom got up, eased the door open and tiptoed into her bedroom. He sat on a chair by the bed. "Are you still lonely?" he said. "Not anymore," said Sarah. "I know you're here."

Tom reached to turn out the light, but she touched his arm. "Please," she said. "May I have a hug?" Smiling, Tom lay down by her side and held her close until she'd fallen asleep. Then, switching out the light, he went back to his room to think over the conversation he'd overheard earlier.

He needed a rescue plan, and fast. He couldn't let Jason down. And the thought of living in a wet cardboard box made him realise how bloody lucky he was. But how could he help? How could he get his hands on the kind of cash his dad needed? Still mulling it over, he fell asleep, drifting into a nightmare where he tried to tell Jason and Mary his story. Who he'd been. Where he'd come from. He was begging them to believe him. They were looking at him and they knew what they were seeing was a troubled teenager, with a vivid imagination, who was probably going to be in therapy for the rest of his life.

Chapter 7

28th December. 6 am.

Tom woke up, confused. He was even more confused when he realised he was back in the white waiting room. The woman in the white flowing dress was standing before him, clipboard in hand. She was over 6ft tall. Only her warm, welcoming smile stopped her from being terrifying.

"What — why am I back here?" he stammered. "What's going on? Am I dead again?"

"No, Tom, no," she said, reassuringly. "I just wanted to check in with you. How is everything going?"

Tom stared at her, still trying to gather his thoughts. After a long pause, he spoke.

"I need to help my dad," he said. "He's a bloody good bloke. Something's going on with this latest build, it's almost like there's something – well, sinister going on. Sounds stupid, but that's my gut instinct. I need to do something about it."

"That's music to my ears," said the woman. Smiling at Tom's puzzled expression, she said: "That's precisely why you were sent back. To help."

"O-kaaay," said Tom. "Care to give me any hints on how?" The woman just shook her head, still smiling. "Sorry Tom, can't help you there."

"Thought not," said Tom, grimly. "But maybe there's something else you could help me with."

"Of course, Tom, if I can."

"I have a bit of a dilemma. I'm in love with a 15-year-old girl. And I'm a 40-year-old man. That's just wrong. It's wrong, right?"

Still smiling, she shook her head. Running her fingers through his hair in a motherly kind of way, she said: "It's not wrong to fall in love, Tom. Remember, you're not a 40-year-old man anymore. You're a 15-year-old boy. You have the memories and skills of an older man, but you're still a 15-year-old boy. So some things you get to do for the first time, and falling in love is one of them. Just don't let it make you forget you have a job to do."

"Fat chance," said Tom. "But thanks, that's helped. Shame you can't sort the rest of it out so easily."

"Trust me, I can only guide you so far," she said. "Because we don't know exactly how things are going to play out. But we know you have the skills and intelligence to figure it out for yourself. I'm confident you will. I have to go now," she added, fading into the white background of the room, with her parting words — "Good luck!" — echoing in his ears.

Tom blinked. He was back in his bedroom. There was a faint knock on his door and Sarah entered, smiling, and sat on his bed. The time was 6.15 am.

"Morning Tom," she said. "Sleep well?"

"Morning Sarah," he answered, still trying to collect his thoughts. "Yes, I — I'm good. How are you?"

"Happy and warm," said Sarah, springing to her feet. "I feel fantastic." She started spinning round and round, laughing, until she fell dizzily down beside Tom. He loved her energy, her spontaneity. And now he saw where she could help him.

Suddenly, he had a vision. A way to re-focus, to reach a brighter future. A way for Jason to build a legacy. But first, he needed coffee. He led Sarah down to the kitchen, where he put the pot on to brew. While Jason and Mary enjoyed a grown-up lie-in, he grabbed some paper and sketched out his ideas to Sarah. "What do you think?" he said. "Be honest."

"I love it Tom," she said, hugging him tightly. "It's amazing. We need to build this, to show how it would work."

"Build it?" said Tom, puzzled.

"A model, dummy!" laughed Sarah. "You've got Lego, right? I saw a big box in your room. We could build an architect's model with it!"

"Brilliant!" said Tom. "You're brilliant! Let's do it!"

Leaving the coffee cups on the counter, they dashed upstairs.

An hour later, Mary popped her head round Tom's door. He and Sarah were busy building some kind of elaborate Lego construction on his bedroom floor. "That looks fantastic!" she said. "What is it?" She smiled to herself — she'd been worried about them being quiet. What brilliant kids.

"Thanks, mum," said Tom. "It's just an idea we're working on. Do you need any help making breakfast?"

"Your dad's making brekkie," she said, grinning. "And you know what he's like in the kitchen. You'd better stay up here."

Sarah's phone beeped as Mary left the room. She frowned as she read the text — it was from George.

"George," she said, in answer to Tom's enquiring look. "He'd like you to come and stay with us at the farm. If you want to."

Sarah never called George 'Dad'. She couldn't stand him. He was a bully, shouting at Lisa and her all the time. At least she couldn't hear his ranting, but it was still scary. He got drunk all the time. One evening he'd even slapped her. Poor Lisa tried to stop him, and got punched in the face. So even though she knew Tom would hate the farm, the freezing, crumbling house, she had to ask him. She didn't want George to punish her.

"Sure," said Tom, probably picking up on some of her thoughts. "I'd like that. It'll mean spending more time with you. But I'll have to run it by my parents, of course."

"Let's ask them over breakfast," said Sarah. "Do you think the roads will be safe today?"

"Yeah, the plough and grit lorries have been out," said Tom. "All the main roads are clear."

Anxious not to keep George waiting, the two went straight downstairs. Mary and Jason agreed – they'd leave in about an hour. It wouldn't be long until Tom found out more about what George was up to. He figured, somewhere in all of Jason's difficulties, George bloody Miller was involved. He didn't know how. But he'd follow his instinct, play the waiting game and work it out.Just over an hour later, Jason drove the kids to the Millers' farmhouse. Tom and Sarah sat in the back and signed to each other on the way.

"I want to make you happy, Sarah."

"You do make me happy."

"I'll never let anyone hurt you ever again. I'm going to protect you. If the bullies pull your hair, I'll punch them. And I'm going to have a quiet word with George. He'll never hurt you again. That's a promise."

"Please, Tom don't get into trouble!"

"It's no trouble. All those bullies have been getting away with things for far too long."

"I might even punch them myself. I want to."

They looked at each other and smiled. Tom hoped the heating was fixed at Miller's home. He didn't want to ask Sarah, but he kept his fingers crossed.

Chapter 8

The Millers' home, Oak Tree Farm, was an old, Tudor-style farmhouse. There was a 'For Sale' sign by the five-bar gate, which had lost several bars and was leaning at a 45-degree angle. A potholed driveway led to the old farmhouse, which had seen better days. The entrance porch was staved in on one side. The paint was peeling from the front door and windows, and two panes were cracked in the widows for the lounge. It was tired, sad, bleak and neglected. It reminded Tom forcibly of the farmhouse of his previous life.

Tom's dad had had a vision. His dream was to own a farm, to live off the land and give his family a good life, like the life he'd had as a boy on his own father's farm. It had been the happiest time of his life. Sadly, his parents — Tom's grandparents — had died in a car crash. He was ripped away to live with his uncle and aunt in Glasgow.

He grew up in the city, met his wife, bought a little terraced house in the city's east end. By this time, he'd found work on the rigs, out in the harsh, cruel, unforgiving North Sea, which meant he was away a lot and only came home for short stays. Together, his mum and dad had saved and saved, his mum working part-time as a cleaner to supplement their income. Eventually, they saved enough to buy a rundown old sheep farm in the Scottish Highlands.

Tom was 8 years old at the time. It felt like an adventure. Sadly, his dad's enthusiasm and commitment couldn't make up for his lack of knowledge about farming and running a business. Tom worked, like his parents, on the farm when he wasn't at school. He tended to the livestock, mended fences, tended the huge vegetable garden at the back of the house. He didn't have friends. He walked or ran to school every day to save money — a 6-mile round trip. Weekends he spent 16 hours a day working alongside his parents. He learned to shoot and in lambing season often took shifts, sitting up all night to guard the tiny animals against foxes and the occasional wildcat. Tom kept guard three nights a week, his dad did four. He had no chance at school, despite his intelligence. He was always too tired to concentrate.

Tom eventually left school at 16 to work full time on the farm. He gave it everything he had, to the point of collapse. Simply because he loved his parents and wanted to help. One winter's day he came in to find his mum cradling his dad on the floor. They didn't have a phone — too expensive. The farm van was broken beyond repair. Tom heard real fear in his mother's voice. "Tom, fetch the doctor," she said. "I think your dad's having a heart attack. Run like the wind, son. Run like the wind."

Tom took the three miles into town flat out. But it was still too late by the time he got back in the doctor's car, his dad was gone. His mum died a year later. She'd simply lost the will to live, and the hard years on the farm had taken their toll. So at 18 years old, Tom was alone in the world with nothing to his name but a non-functional farm and a mountain of debt.

He'd never sell it. It was home — not to mention that no one in their right mind would want to buy it. There was no mortgage to pay. In retrospect, maybe the fact that it was so cheap when his parents bought it outright should have been a warning. But there were still debts to settle from suppliers and a business loan to pay off from the bank. He packed a bag and made his way back to Glasgow, got a job on a building site, labouring 12 hours a day, seven days a week and lived in a battered caravan on-site. Each month he put most of his wages towards paying off his debts. It was going to take at least ten years, but he was determined. All the same, he was becoming an angry, sad and lonely teenager. Everyone on site left him alone. He kept his head down and worked hard.

One evening, in the site canteen, he watched an old 1973 movie: *Day of the Jackal*, starring Edward Fox. Fox was playing an assassin who attempts, for an extremely large sum of money, to kill the French president. It gave him an idea. Maybe there was another way.

Jason parked his Range Rover outside the old farmhouse. George's car wasn't there. Lisa's beat-up, rusty Ford Focus was parked in the driveway, covered in snow.

"Have a great day, Tom," he said, as the two kids climbed from the vehicle. "Sarah, it's been a real pleasure meeting you. Tom, if you want me to pick you up later or tomorrow, just phone."

"Thanks, Dad," said Tom, waving from the driveway

"Thanks, Jason," said Sarah, shyly. "I've had the best time."

Tom and Sarah went into the farmhouse kitchen along a hall with a carpet only fit for burning. There were damp patches and mould on the walls, and the wallpaper was peeling away. No wonder Sarah hated the farm, thought Tom. It was bloody freezing — probably warmer outside. What a shithole.

Lisa was in the back yard, trying to chop old wooden pallets into firewood, desperate to warm the house. Tom and Sarah saw her from the kitchen window. "I don't know where George is," signed Sarah. "Sorry. I have to go and help her."

"Look, I'll go and send her in," said Tom. "I'll chop the wood and get the home fires burning. You look after Lisa, okay?"

"Thanks, Tom," she said. "I'm so glad you're here. Poor Lisa looks worn out."

Tom picked up the empty log baskets and went outside, memories of doing the same thing many years before, on the farm, flooding his head. Surreal. He shook his head. Where was bloody George? He managed to keep a lid on his anger. "Hello, Mrs. Miller," he said, gently. "Please go inside — you look frozen. I'll take care of this, and Sarah will make you a hot drink."

Lisa didn't have enough strength to argue. "Thanks, Tom," she said. "You're a good boy. I could certainly do with a hand. Hello, Sarah," she went on, seeing her adopted daughter come outside. "Did you have a good time?"

"I had a great time, thanks," said Sarah, taking her arm. "Come on inside. You look tired. I'll make you some cocoa and get you a blanket." The two went back inside, while Tom attacked the spiky boards with the hatchet. With a full basket of fuel, he went inside and got the stove going, before heading back out to chop some more. Sarah made Lisa a mug of cocoa and put a blanket around her shoulders. By the time George got home, the kitchen was warm from the stove and the log basket was full. Sarah had soup on the go. It was all memory lane to Tom. The aroma of the soup, his mum in the kitchen as he came in, after working long, exhausting hours. He smiled at Sarah.

George sat by the kitchen table, a tumbler of whiskey in his lazy, smooth politician hand. Tom looked into the man's brown eyes, wondering what voters would think of his home situation. Throwing Tom one of his best false smiles, George thanked him for sorting the firewood. "I had an important meeting this morning," he said. "Government work never stops; you know?" Tom nodded, thinking the man was full of shit. "Have you been back to the club since Boxing Day?" George went on. "We were all very impressed with your performance, young man. Hey, maybe after lunch you could show me some more of your shooting skills. Just a bit of fun, eh? What do you say?"

"Sounds like a plan, Mr Miller," answered Tom, turning his attention to Sarah. "Wow, Sarah, that soup smells good. I'm hungry as a horse!"

"That's some scar on your face," said George, rudely. "How did you get it?"

"Long story, Mr Miller," replied Tom, yawning. God, if he had a pound for every time someone asked him that question, he'd have no problems in this world. Sarah, who'd been watching them talk, smiled at her friend, understanding his frustration. Lisa hardly said a word, lost in her own sad world. Sitting round the table, eating Sarah's delicious soup and sharing the bread, Tom couldn't help thinking about the last supper.

Chapter 9

Lunch over, Tom and George put their coats on and went out for a walk. 400m from the house and away from prying eyes, George stopped by a ladder leaning against an old tree. "Okay Tom," he said, smirking. "If you climb up and face due north, you'll see a target. Up to you, of course, just a bit of fun..."

"Sure," said Tom. "Like you say, just a bit of fun. But why do you want to see me shoot again? You've seen me plenty of times before at the club."

"I wanted to see you shoot outside. Give you a bit of a test, you know, see how good you really are." Slapping Tom heartily on the back, he handed over a rifle bag and four bullets, his little piggy eyes gleaming. Tom nodded and climbed the ladder. Reaching a thick branch facing in the right direction, he quickly opened the bag and loaded the rifle. He lay along the branch and looked through the telescopic sights. Jesus Christ. George Miller was a first-class prick. No imagination. No wonder the country was in a bloody mess.

A watermelon sat on top of a rickety old shed, eyes, a nose and a mouth painted on in white, dribbly paint. A trilby hat sat on top of the whole sad thing. The paint running from the eyes made the melon look like it was crying. Tom couldn't blame it. It was about 300m away.

The rifle was ancient, filthy and poorly-kept, a one-shot model, probably bought by the farm's original owner and largely ignored since the farm went out of commission. What a joke. Tom let out a deep sigh. Now he knew exactly what old George wanted from him. His shooting skills. George put binoculars to his eyes, watching like a hawk. "Hat first, I think, Tom," he called.

Tom slowed his breathing, aimed and gently squeezed. The trilby hat flew into the air. Tom reloaded.

"Well done!" shouted George. "Now try for the eyes. Just for fun, just for fun," George chortled.

Tom started to really feel uncomfortable. Sweat formed on his brow. *Give it your best shot Tom*, he said to himself, keeping down the anger. He aimed, fired, reloaded, fired. "Bloody well done!" shouted George. "Both eyes out!"

Tom dropped the rifle. It hit the snow-covered ground by George's feet, making him jump. He grinned, dropped the bag and climbed down the ladder with two things on his mind. Who was the target? And how much money was this amateur going to offer?

In his previous life, Tom had been the most wanted criminal on this planet. A meticulous planner, he'd never been caught. He was the best. He was The Eagle assassin. But he'd never met face-to-face with a client. This was icy ground, and not just because of the packed snow. One thing he knew — George was a desperate man, or he wouldn't be getting a 15-year-old boy involved, even one with Tom's skills. George had sold his soul on his quest to become Prime Minister.

Tom walked alongside George, waiting for him to speak. "Well, boy," said George, at last. "I know your dad's latest build isn't going to plan, and he's short of cash. I might have a way for you to help him. I know a lot of influential people... all I need is for you to do me a small favour. That's not much to ask, to save your dad's business, is it?"

Tom glared at George, coughed and spoke. The voice came from the past. Deep, menacing. And Glaswegian. "Cut to the chase George," he growled. "We both know what you want. And we both know it'll cost."

George froze. Who was this kid? He was only going to use him as a backup, to make sure his plan was foolproof, but it seemed like he was something other than he appeared. George steadied himself by placing his hands on the fence until he'd regained his composure enough to speak, albeit with a slight quiver in his voice. "How... how much?" he managed.

Tom had him over a barrel, and they both knew it. Mr Deputy Prime Minister had just admitted his intention. He'd played his trump card too early. And his whole hand was weak. It was all damage limitation now.

Still in that deep Scottish accent, Tom spoke briskly. "Okay George, here's the deal. I'll supply my services on three conditions. One: afterwards, you don't try to stop me seeing Sarah. Two: stop fucking around with my dad's business, because now I know it's you. Three: 50k in cash up front. Call it goodwill. In fact, let's make it four conditions. And George, this one's important. No one, I repeat no one, will ever know who you hired. With me so far?"

George was in a trance-like state, not believing what he was hearing. Suddenly Tom was calling all the shots, and it should be the other way around. Tom glanced towards the farmhouse, thinking of Sarah and Lisa. He loaded the rifle with its last bullet, and pointed it at George. It took every ounce of his self-control not to squeeze the trigger.

"Here's something else to think about," he snarled. "If you ever lay another fucking finger on Sarah or Lisa, I'll blow your fucking brains out and piss on your fucking grave. You sick, weak, bastard. Call yourself a man? Beating kids and women? See George, Sarah and I don't have any secrets. She's told me all... about... you..."

George was literally shaking in his boots. Suddenly, Tom saw movement in his peripheral vision. Sarah was slowly making her way towards them. He unloaded the weapon, placed it against the fence and handed the bullet to George with a meaningful look.

He waved at Sarah, and signed: "Hi! George and I were just having a nice chat and some shooting practice. Weren't we, George?"

"I've set the chessboard up," signed Sarah. "Come back inside, it's warm by the fire and I've made more cocoa."

"Sounds great!" Tom signed back. "Although George might want something stronger — a brandy, perhaps."

George had never bothered to learn sign language, and had no idea why the two were laughing. Tom yanked his arm, saying: "Come on, Mr Miller! You look frozen, we don't want you to catch your death... yet." Picking up the rifle and stowing it back in its bag, he smiled and took Sarah's outstretched hand. They left George dragging along behind them as they walked back to the house.

Back at the Drake house, Jason was sitting in his recliner, trying to relax. He still had rainy day money in his safe. It was about 40k, meant to provide for Mary and Tom if anything happened to him. He couldn't bring himself to use it, not to save his business. Mary, meanwhile, was in Tom's room, emptying his washing basket. The drawing pad was on his desk, the Lego build still on the floor. She looked at them both. Looked again. "Jason!" she called out, a sense of urgency in her voice. "JASON!"

"What is it? What's wrong?" shouted Jason, racing up the stairs. Mary held out the drawing pad. "You'd better sit down and take a look at this," she said. The title on the top, in bold letters, read: "THE FUTURE OF BUILDING HOMES."

Back at the farm, Sarah and Tom played chess by the fire. Lisa sat quietly in the corner of the lounge. George was in his bedroom. He prised up a floorboard and pulled out a bag stuffed with cash, a private hoard he was keeping for a personal rainy day. Lisa and Sarah knew nothing about it, and never would.

He pulled out two wedges, making up the £50k Tom had demanded. Placing them on Tom's bed, and dropping a couple of books on top with a growl, he headed downstairs. "I've, er, put those books we were talking about on your bed," he said.

"Thanks!" said Tom, with infuriating brightness. "That's very kind of you!"

Chapter 10

Tom didn't bother making eye contact with George. His eyes were on Sarah; it was time to get her out of this dump. Lisa Miller was an adult and, as far as he was concerned, could look out for herself. He wasn't sure how he could help her. Sarah, on the other hand, was his best friend. He'd do anything for her. He had to focus on her. He really felt sorry for Lisa, but she could leave if she chose. In fact, Tom couldn't understand why she stayed.

George sat in the lounge, as far away from Tom as he could get. Just 5ft 6in tall, he weighed over 14 stone. He was 42 years old, grey hair, a big beer belly, horribly unfit. He drank too much, blamed it on the pressure of his job. His only interest was in getting to the top and watching the money roll in. He was a selfish man, mixed up with a lot of corrupt and powerful people. Until now, he'd thought he was in control.

Tom thought about George as he played chess with Sarah. A small pawn in a much bigger game. Countries weren't run by politicians. Countries were run by large businesses, by people with money. The rich ruled the world, that was the system. Politicians were just puppets on a string, and the rich were the puppeteers who did anything they wanted to line their own pockets.

Sarah signed, so she didn't disturb Lisa, who'd drifted into a doze. Also so George wouldn't understand their conversation. He was sitting, glaring at Tom. She shivered. She truly hated the man. "I'm glad you came today," she signed. "I feel safer when you're here."

"George won't be hurting either of you ever again," Tom signed back. "I've had a word."

"I thought he looked shaken," replied Sarah, stifling a giggle. Tom grinned. "Tell you what," he signed. "Let's go back to mine. Then you don't need to think about him at all."

"Yes, please," answered Sarah. "I hate it here. George is always drunk, the house is always freezing — I feel so sorry for Lisa, but I've begged her to leave, and she won't listen. I don't know what else to do."

"I know," he signed. "Not much you can do. Let me phone my dad. He'll come and pick us up."

Jason's cheerful consent sent the two of them scurrying off to collect their things. Tom came back down first. George was in the kitchen, drinking whisky again. Tom leaned over his shoulder, and hissed in his ear. "Sarah's coming to stay with me, for as long as she wants to," he said. "She shouldn't be living in this shithole. This is non-negotiable."

George nodded and sipped his whisky. "Right," said Tom. "Who's the target and when's the hit? I need to plan." The alcohol had loosened George's tongue, given him some Dutch courage. Tom stared out of the window, while the man spoke, because if he looked at him, he'd lose control and pummel his fucking face in.

"The PM, you little shit," George hissed. "New Year's Eve fireworks, London Eye. Midnight. And remember, son, you're just a kid. No-one would believe you if you tried to grass me up."

"Okay George," said Tom, calmly. "And thanks for the cash. Oh, and for the record: I think you're a fucking madman. And I'm not your son. If I was your son, I'd fucking shoot myself. You're just another fucking slimeball politician. One day, I promise you, I'll piss on your fucking grave."

George's hands were shaking and sweat was pouring from his brow. But he was out of smart answers. Instead, he refilled his glass from the bottle in front of him. 25-year-old Macallan, Tom noted. Fifteen hundred quid a bottle. How could the man sit there drinking expensive whisky while his wife and daughter had holes in their shoes and threadbare coats? George was a fucking arsehole.

Going into the lounge, to Lisa, now awake, who was standing by the fire, he said, gently: "Are you okay, Mrs. Miller? Can I fetch you more wood or get you anything? I'd like to help you, if I can."

Lisa turned and smiled. What a lovely boy, and so handsome. No wonder Sarah was head over heels with him. He reminded her of her first husband, a true gentleman. Sadly, this was her life now. But she'd made her own bed, there was no one else to blame.

"I'm fine, Tom," she said, smiling sadly. "I'm just tired. I'll be okay once I've had a good night's sleep. And you have helped, so much. I'm so glad Sarah has a friend like you."

"I'm taking her back to mine for a few days," he said. "You know she'll be well looked after there. You don't mind, do you?"

"No, Tom," she said, taking his hand. "That's fine by me. I just want her to be happy."

"You could come too," Tom said. "I know my folks would be happy to have you, and we have plenty of room."

"Thanks, Tom," Lisa replied. "But — I have things to do here. I need to get my house in order. Just... just look after Sarah. That's all I ask."

There was something going on there, Tom was sure. But it was out of his hands. He gave Lisa a hug and a peck on the cheek, squeezed her cold hands and nodded. Sarah would be well looked after, he could guarantee it.

Twenty minutes later, Jason pulled up outside the farmhouse and beeped the horn. Sarah gave Lisa a long hug while Tom ran ahead to open the car doors. "What a little gent," Lisa thought, watching her daughter skip down the drive, watching them all wave goodbye as they drove away.

Chapter 11

"How about we all go out tonight?" said Mary, when they were all together again.

"Great idea!" replied Jason. "I'll call Luigi's. Seven o'clock?"

Mary nodded her agreement, while Tom signed the plan to Sarah. "Come on," he said, speaking clearly as he reached for her hand. "Let's get changed – it's dead posh at Luigi's!" He dragged her up the stairs behind him, excited. This was their first date! He'd worry about George's assignment later on.

An hour later, dressed for the occasion. Tom and Sarah sat in the kitchen, waiting for the adults. Tom had his grey suit on, polished black shoes, a white shirt, and a navy blue tie. Sarah was wearing her favourite — and only — dress. Red, flared at the hip to fall in pretty folds that swished and swirled about her when she moved. Her hair was up in a glossy bun to show off her gold chain. Even her school shoes looked nice, polished by Tom while she was dressing.

"Our first date!" she signed to him, laughing. "I'm excited!"

"Me too," replied Tom. "I'm buzzing more than a bumblebee!"

"You look really cool," signed Sarah.

"Well, you look amazing," answered Tom.

Sarah touched her gold chain and smiled. She couldn't believe her luck.

Jason popped his head around the door. "Are you hungry?"

"SO hungry!" replied Tom, dashing to fetch Sarah's coat.

All of them were in high spirits as they travelled to the restaurant, where the friendly maître d' showed them to their table. Tom and Sarah sat opposite Jason and Mary, so Sarah could lip-read. Tom had it all planned out.

A waitress brought over the menus. "Would you like anything to drink?" she asked. "Yes please," said Tom, in an important voice. "Two large bottles of your finest sparkling mineral water. We're celebrating, you see. It's my first date with Sarah. She's my girlfriend."

The waitress nodded, clearly trying not to chuckle. "Certainly sir," she said. "Please just call me over when you're ready to order."

Tom checked the prices, he didn't want this meal to break the bank. "Hey look," he said. "We're in time for the pre-theatre set meal. Looks good, doesn't it?"

"Yes it does," Mary replied, looking a little relieved. "That will be perfect." Sarah grasped Tom's hand and held it tight. He was such a gentleman, so confident and at ease. She'd struck gold. After they'd ordered, Sarah lifted her glass to Jason and Mary. "Thank you both," she said. "I'm so grateful to you for having me to stay."

"We love having you," said Mary. "You're welcome to stay for as long as you want." Everyone round the table beamed at each other.

After an excellent meal, and an excellent first date for the young couple, they headed home. Jason got some coffee on the go for him and Mary, some cocoa for Tom and Sarah. The two young people headed upstairs, came back carrying the board on which they'd built their Lego village between them. They placed it on the coffee table, while Jason and Mary sat on the sofa and listened to their plans, Tom talking and Sarah displaying the sketches on his command. After 20 minutes, he was almost done. "This is the future of housing, I think," he said. "It'll leave a legacy for others to follow, a new style of living. It could be built on 35-40 acres of land. Think about it, Dad. It could be our flagship, our starting point. We could see villages like this built across the nation. What do you think?"

The room was silent. It was a lot of information to take in. Tom had spent hours and hours on this project, in his former life. It was a way of passing the evenings in that cold caravan on the building site. He'd hoped to be a good man, once. He'd had real passion for this project, real belief in it. He hoped he could make it work this time round.

He could see the idea sending up sparks in Jason's brain. He knew it was taking hold, that his new father was the man to make it happen. He nodded to himself, satisfied for that day.

"Okay, it's a lot," he said. "Why don't we leave you in peace to think it over — it's past bedtime anyway. So goodnight, both of you. And thanks for a wonderful day."

Hugs and kisses all around, and Tom and Sarah headed upstairs. "What do you think?" he asked. "Could it work?" Sarah nodded, firmly. "Absolutely," she signed. "It was awesome. You were awesome. I think they loved it. I can't wait to hear what they say tomorrow."

Downstairs, Jason and Mary were deep in conversation. Tom's presentation had blown their minds. So thought through. Such a talented boy. They looked at the Lego model.

It was so simple — rows and rows of terraced houses, but with a modern twist. Village living in an urban setting, with every development complete with its own shops, crèches, cafés, and restaurants, pubs, village halls — everything the residents could need. Local 'police' stations, manned 24/7 by security teams, to keep people safe. Roads took second place to space for kids to play, planned so people could access their homes and amenities but still let their children play in safety.

Every house had a decent-sized back garden, with plenty of room for a conservatory or extension to provide added space. It was all based on the community spirit Tom had experienced growing up, the spirit that saw everyone look out for everyone else, before houses were torn down to make way for massive, sad-looking, concrete high-rise blocks. The town planners who came up with those should have been shot at dawn.

One by one, slowly and methodically, Jason and Mary scanned Tom's sketches. They both felt it was sensational, beyond words. They were excited, inspired. The passion was back. "It's so simple," said Jason, "But so brilliant. I'll need to speak to Bill Brown in the new year, he's a bloody good architect. I'm sure we can make this happen. How did the boy come up with this? I'm bloody amazed!"

"I'm with you," laughed Mary. "The concept is fantastic. You know what? I think you should phone Bill right now. Go on. I'll go and check on the kids."

Tom and Sarah were ready for bed and waiting for Mary to say goodnight. She went to Sarah's room first. "Got everything you need?" she asked, taking care to enunciate clearly and let Sarah see her lips. When the girl nodded from her snug pillow, she wished her goodnight and went through to see Tom. She gave her boy a hug, sat back on his bed and smiled.

"Dad's going to give Bill Brown a call," she said. "He's the best architect we know. We're so impressed, Tom." Tom beamed up at her. She kissed his forehead. "Night son," she said. "I love you."

"Night mum. Love you too."

Mary turned the light off and closed the door. Tom grinned to himself. Bill Brown was the perfect man for this job. He closed his eyes and listened to his mum's footsteps as she went downstairs. His phone buzzed with the expected text.

Thanks for today, Tom. Our first date was magical. Where are we going on our second?

I'm going to surprise you.

I can't wait!

Are you lonely tonight?

Not tonight, thanks to you. I feel safe and warm.

Night Sarah, sleep well.

Night Tom. Love you. xxx

Tom: Oops, sorry, kisses! Love you too. xxx

Sarah, by the light of her lamp, opened her diary.

Dear Clare. I wish you were here, so we could share moments like these. I still think of you, mum and dad every day. You were the best sister. I'm not even angry with you anymore for stealing my stuff to buy drugs. We all make mistakes, that's how we learn and grow. I've made plenty, but I'm still going. I wish I could change the past, but I can't. I have to keep moving forward, not back. I believe I have a real chance now to live a good life with Tom. I want to tell you some great news. My first date with Tom. We went to a restaurant — first time ever for me!! It was brilliant, I nearly cried, I was so happy. Tom told the waitress I was his girlfriend. His GIRLFRIEND! Whoop whoop! So I know he loves me. He's so handsome, Clare. He makes the sun come out for me, even on rainy days. And he's had troubles too. He was homeless for a while, nobody's sure how. He says he has amnesia, so whatever happened must have been really bad. But now we have each other. We have so much in common, so much fun. I think we're both trying to relive our lost childhoods. It's brilliant. I feel so happy, I could burst. I just wish you were here. I love you and I miss you.

Tom waited until the household was asleep. He got up and carefully went downstairs, George's cash in his hand. He'd stashed £5k in Sarah's bag earlier that night and now, dialling the combination to the safe, he opened it and put another £5k inside. He'd do the same thing every couple of months, and hide the rest in his private drawer. He had it all planned. He thought about it as he got back in bed. The more he thought, the more he understood why he'd been sent back. No point dwelling on the past. That was gone and he didn't miss it one bit. He was here to build a future.

Chapter 12

29th December.

Sarah was up and downstairs before Tom next morning. Mary was already in the kitchen, setting about breakfast for four. She smiled as she saw Sarah come in. She didn't want to pry into the Millers' finances, but the poor kid, holes in her shoes. Mary felt the need to spoil the girl. If Sarah agreed, she'd take her shopping.

After a morning hug, Sarah asked if she could help make breakfast. "Of course!" said Mary. "Us girls have to stick together, right? You lay the table, I'll get the bacon on the go. We'll work as a team." Jason and Tom came downstairs a short time later to a full English breakfast — a great start to a new day. Mary was on a mission, excited. While Jason and Tom cleaned the kitchen, she turned to Sarah. "Would you like to come shopping with me today?" she asked. "I have a load of gift vouchers Jason bought me, so we could shop til we drop. It'd be so much fun."

Sarah's face lit up. "Yes please, Mary, that would be awesome!" she said. They left the men to their task and went to get ready. Jason went to his safe to get some extra cash for Mary. He knew what she had planned — he'd noticed Sarah's shoes and threadbare coat too. He put the cash in Mary's hand, feeling good about it. It was the right thing to do. Mary and an excited Sarah left for their shopping trip, Jason headed for his study, and Tom went upstairs to his books.

His phone lit up. Withheld number. He knew who it was. Switching to his Glaswegian voice, he answered: "Hi George. What can I do for you today?"

"It's all set for New Year's Eve," came George's harsh voice. "The PM's going to launch the fireworks at the London Eye. There's a rifle hidden on top of the escalator at your dad's new build. Don't shoot until he presses the button. Do I make myself clear?"

"Crystal," Tom replied. The line went dead.

A few hours later, Tom's phone lit up again. A more welcome sight this time — a text from Sarah.

Hope you're not feeling too lonely!

I'm fine, Sarah. Having fun?

So much fun! I thought I was going to help Mary chose her clothes, but *she's* bought *me* loads of stuff! I'm blown away!

Brilliant! What have you bought?

Loads of things. I'll show you later. We'll be home in about an hour. x

See you then.☺ xxx

Tom spent the hour on his laptop, learning everything he could about the New Year's Eve firework display. Whether the Eye would be operational. Where the crowds would be, where the PM would be standing and who would be standing beside him. His ideal position, sight lines, angles, weather conditions. The streets would be packed with revellers. It was vital that no-one else got hurt.

He heard his mum's car pull into the driveway, closed the laptop and ran down to greet them. "Woah!" he said, as they struggled through the door with their bags. "Looks like you two need a hand!"

"We had so much fun!" said Mary, panting as she dropped her bags in the hallway.

"We really did," said Sarah. "The shops were packed. Mary had to hold my hand to make sure I didn't get lost in the crowd. We got some amazing bargains — my coat and shoes were half price!" Sarah blushed and smiled at Tom, who smiled back as he helped them both carry their bags upstairs. In Sarah's room, she showed off her new things. "I'm so lucky Tom," she signed, as she twirled in her new coat. "I feel like Cinderella. But Mary spent loads of money on me, I don't how I'll ever pay her back. I'll find a way, though. I will."

"There's no need, Sarah, really," said Tom. "I can see how much Mum loved doing it. So you've kind of paid her back already!" Besides, he thought to himself. I know Dad gave Mum money from the safe. So good old George actually treated his daughter right, for the first time in his life, even if he didn't know it. Two new pairs of shoes and a pair of pink wellies. A new winter coat. Two pairs of jeans, several snuggly jumpers, pyjamas, slippers, bed socks, and two new dresses. He'd have a fit. Shame he didn't know, really.

At Oak Tree Farm, Lisa Miller was deep in thought. George would be home later. He'd changed so much since they married, from being okay into a total bastard, a nasty, evil, manipulative, violent man. She didn't have a clue why. All she knew was that neither she nor Sarah could stand him anymore.

She'd still been grieving when she first met George. He'd been a friend of her late husband, although she hadn't known him. He'd swept her off her feet, so kind and generous, so sympathetic. He'd convinced her he was a good man and that he loved her. They married within a year. She'd bought the farmhouse with her savings and the life insurance from her husband's death. They would fix it up together, make it a home. He persuaded her they should adopt a child. She was reluctant at first, but then she met Sarah, and fell instantly in love. But it was all for show. She was a pretty wife, Sarah was a pretty girl. They looked good for press photos at political functions or ribbon-cuttings at the village fete. Other than that, George didn't care about them. He didn't care about anyone but himself. He'd promised her the world, and delivered nothing. It was her own fault. What else did she expect from a bloody politician?

Lisa was trying to pluck up the courage to leave. But George had beaten all the confidence out of her. She was a bad mother, a terrible wife. She'd let herself go. Her hair was grey and knotted, she'd lost a stone in weight. She never bothered with makeup anymore. She stopped going to the Leisure Centre and dropped Sarah off to school early, so no one would see her. She was depressed, lonely, desperate. She'd have ended it all, if it hadn't been for Sarah. But meeting Tom, Mary, and Jason had helped her make her mind up. Sarah would be taken care of. She had freedom to act.

She knew George was trying to get Tom involved in whatever his latest promotion scheme was. Lisa knew a hell of a lot about George, and all his underhand dealings. All of it written down, in detail, with emails, bank statements, photos of her injuries and copies of medical records, anything that would offer proof. She looked at the bulky envelope she'd stashed everything in and nodded. She'd do it tonight, show Sarah how much she cared. Set them both free. For the first time in ages, she felt good. This was the right thing to do.

She sent a text to Sarah.

Hello love, sorry to bother you. Just wanted to know you are okay and having fun, and to say that I put some money in your bag, in case you need to buy anything. Maybe new shoes and a coat? Love you. x

With plenty of time on her hands, Lisa took a shower, blow-dried her hair properly. Even put on some makeup and did her nails. She glanced at her watch —George would be home any minute. She turned to the wardrobe, smiling, and reached for her dress. Her wedding dress. The first one. The one she'd worn on the happiest day of her life. She still remembered the smile on her husband-to-be's handsome face as she walked down the aisle. She couldn't believe, remembering it, that she'd ever married George. She'd never even voted for the man.

Chapter 13

Back at the Drake's everyone was getting ready to go out for a snowy walk in the park. Now that Sarah had some proper winter gear, it was time for them all to get some fresh air. Her phone buzzed as she sat at the bottom of the stairs, pulling on her new pink wellies. She read Lisa's text and replied.

Hi Lisa, I'm having a great time, thanks! Thank you so much for the money, that's so kind of you. How are you? I can come back, if you're feeling lonely. Remember there's soup in the fridge. Stay warm and text me if you need anything. x

They went for a long walk. Tom and Sarah ran around in the park, laughing and joking, not a care in the world. The adults joined in a friendly snowball fight. Real family fun. They got home before darkness fell, lit the fire in the lounge and made hot drinks. Sarah was so deliriously happy, she forgot about the money in her bag.

Mary had a treat for them today. Marshmallows, for toasting over the fire. As Jason and Sarah picked out a movie for everyone to watch, Tom set three of the smoking sweets on her plate. "Watch out!" he signed, when she came back to join him. "It's hot, hot, hot, so don't burn your tongue!"

She smiled and put the plate by her side. "Thanks, Tom," she said. "I'll be careful." They sat together on the floor, holding hands and watching the movie, a plate of marshmallows in front of them. Suddenly, Tom felt dizzy. He started sweating. A shiver ran down his spine and a tight band seemed to form around his chest. He was fighting for breath. "Oh no!" he thought, "I'm going to have another heart attack! No, please, don't do this to me..." His hands were shaking as he keeled over, unconscious, to the horror of the three people who loved him most.

Sarah screamed, still holding his hand. Mary reacted quickest. She checked him out, he had a pulse. Keeping her composure — Tom needed her! — she moved him into the recovery position. Jason had already dialled emergency services, an ambulance was on the way.

Mary tried to comfort a hysterical Sarah "He'll be okay, he'll be okay," Mary repeated, to herself as much as Sarah. The girl held Tom's hand tight and wouldn't let go, even when the paramedics arrived. Tom was stretchered into the ambulance, Sarah was still holding on for dear life. Mary and Sarah got into the ambulance. Jason followed in his car, his face old and grey. "Be okay, Tom," he muttered. "Please, be okay."

Like Mary, Jason was trying to stay calm, to think positive, to fight the sickening feeling in his stomach. He gripped the steering wheel and focused on the drive to the hospital, parked the car and raced to join his family.

Sarah and Mary were huddled together in the A&E waiting area. Sarah looked at Jason. She'd calmed down, but was angry with the doctors and the nurses. "They made me let go of his hand," she said. "They made me let go. But he'll be fine," she added, fiercely. "He'd never leave us.

Never!" Jason sat and put his arms around them both. All they could do was wait.

An agonising couple of hours later, a young, stressed-out looking doctor came up to them. "We've got him stabilised," he said, before anyone could speak. "He's being well looked after while we run some tests. Does he have any food allergies or anything? Anything else you can think of?"

Mary shook her head. "Can we see him?" she asked. "Please, we need to see him."

Lisa stood in the hallway, waiting for her husband, wedding gown flowing, gun in her hand. As George opened the front door, she fired. The force of the double-barrel shotgun pellets lifted him off of his feet and blew him back outside. He lay on his back in the snow, a look of shock and horror on his face, blood pouring from his wound. He looked like a beached whale, with his big beer belly. Lisa walked towards him, shotgun ready. She stood over him, glared with utter contempt.

"Hello George," she said, aiming once again. "I've been meaning to tell you... I want a divorce." She hardly heard the roar as she squeezed the trigger.

She dropped the weapon on George's body and stepped back inside. She went into the lounge, where the fire was crackling with the last of the wood Tom had cut for her. She'd been saving it. The heat felt good. She made a call to the police, feeling like she was having an out-of-body experience. Feeling good for the first time in ten years. She'd done it for Sarah. It didn't matter what happened to her. She'd done the right thing. Sarah was safe now. Lisa had finally put her house in order.

The fat envelope containing all her notes, her corroboration, was neatly placed on the kitchen table, along with and all of George's online passwords. He'd used the dark web to hire an assassin. An assassin! Who did he think he was — James Bond? She snorted out a laugh as the sound of sirens came into hearing.

Tom opened his eyes. The woman in white stood before him. He was back in the waiting room. He stayed silent, feeling confused and angry. "Hello Tom," she said. "Sorry about all the theatre. We don't have much time."

"What sort of game are you playing?" he snapped. "Why am I back here? What. Is. Going. On?"

"Please Tom, you need to calm down," she said. "No need to wake the dead!" She smiled at her own feeble joke, then sighed. She never had fun these days. It was all work, work, work. "Anyway," she went on with an embarrassed cough. "I got you here to warn you. Sarah's going to need your help. Will you help her?"

"Of course I will!" Tom barked. "I'll help her any way I can. I love her!"

The woman looked relieved. "I have to tell you," she said. "Grave danger is on the way. I can't stop it, I wish I could. It's all tied up with you, and your family, and George and Sarah. It's too complicated to get into specifics, but here's what you need to know..."

Chapter 14

Tom sat up and coughed out a half-eaten marshmallow.

"Are you okay?" said a startled nurse. "I'll fetch a doctor," she added, scurrying out.

Tom surveyed his surroundings. He didn't like hospitals one bit. It was the smell, that strange odour, neither life nor death, some kind of tightrope between the two. Minutes later, a young doctor appeared, looking harassed and worn out. He raised his eyebrows and shook his head as he saw the half-eaten marshmallow on the bed. Where the hell had that come from? Tom's airways had been checked several times. This had just appeared like magic.

"Er... how are you feeling?" the doctor asked. "You coughed up a marshmallow? Where did that come from?"

Tom shrugged, trying to look puzzled. "No idea," he said, "I can't really remember anything. I feel great now though, never better. Can I see my mum and dad? And Sarah?"

"Let's check your stats first," said the doctor, producing a stethoscope and applying it to Tom's chest. The nurse was already fastening the cuff of a blood pressure reader to his upper arm, and checking his blood oxygen stats on the monitors above him. After five minutes, the doctor sat back. He and the nurse exchanged confused looks.

"Well, I can't explain it," he said. "Everything checks out. I don't know how we missed that bloody marshmallow, though... I'll go and get your family." He headed out of the door, scratching his head. Next minute, Sarah was jumping on the bed, crushing him with a hug, and Jason and Mary were bending over him, grinning anxiously. Mary hugged him. "You gave us quite a fright," she said.

"I wouldn't let go of your hand!" Sarah burst in. "Two nurses had to drag me away. I didn't want to let go, I knew you'd be okay if I kept hold of your hand."

Jason was silent, just breathing deeply. "I'm sorry you all got such a fright," said Tom. "I can't believe I nearly choked on a toasted marshmallow. I guess too much sugar really is bad for your health!"

An hour later, they were on their way home. Mary had to keep wiping her tears. Sarah handed Tom his phone, texted him.

Are you really okay?

Yeah. Sorry about all that.

Don't be sorry. First time in an ambulance for me.

Did they have a siren and flashing lights on?

Yes, like in the movies. I was so scared.

I'm sorry

It's okay. I knew you'd be okay. I knew you'd never leave us.

That's for sure, not without a fight.

I wouldn't let go of your hand. Could you feel me holding on?

I think I did. Thanks, Sarah. You probably saved my life.

I love you, Tom.

I love you too.

Jason turned into the driveway. A police car and another car were parked outside the house. "What now?" he thought. "Haven't we had enough drama for one day?"

"Get the kids inside, Mary," he said. "I'll find out what's going on."

Jason suddenly thought about all his outstanding parking tickets. Were they here to arrest him? That would be embarrassing. Tom bit his lower lip and held Sarah's hand. He guessed it was something to do with Lisa and George. How bad was it? They'd find out soon enough.

"Whatever it is," he signed, as they sat together in the lounge, "We'll face it together."

Outside, a young woman was showing Jason her ID. "I'm Detective Sergeant Susan Collins," she said. "This is Judith Winters, from social services. Are you Mr. Jason Drake?"

"Yes," said Jason, hesitantly. "What's this about?"

"Do you think we could come inside, sir?" she asked.

"Of— of course!" he stammered, ushering them into the house and out of the cold.

They all gathered in the lounge. "I'm afraid we have some bad news," said DS Collins, looking round them all until her gaze landed on Sarah. "Are you Sarah Miller, miss?"

"This is Sarah," said Mary, sitting beside the girl and taking her other hand. "What's this all about? Are George and Lisa okay?"

Collins shook her head. "I'm really sorry to tell you this, Miss," she said, quietly. "George Miller died earlier this evening." Sarah gasped, but said nothing. Everyone else stared at the detective. "I'm afraid he was shot... by Mrs. Lisa Miller." There was no point sugar-coating it. It'd be on the news later— the shooting, the letter, the revelations about Miller's activities. But one step at a time.

Sarah was shaking. Jason was pacing the room. "This can't be right," he said. "Lisa, shoot George? No, this can't be right."

"Did Lisa admit it?" asked Mary, squeezing Sarah's hand. "Surely there's some mistake? Lisa wouldn't shoot anyone, let alone her husband. She'd never abandon Sarah like this. I can't believe it."

"There is more to the story," Collins replied. "But I can't share it with you right now. My job is just to tell you the basics, and take care of Sarah."

"Wait — is that why you're here?" Jason demanded, pointing to the woman from social services. "You can't seriously be thinking of taking Sarah away? And to where? A kids' home? Over my dead body! The girl needs our support. The best place for her is right here, with people who love and care for her!"

"Jason's right," said Mary. "Sarah's safe here. She needs us. Please, please don't think about taking her away."

Judith Winters sighed. "Please try to stay calm," she said, not unkindly. "I have to do my job here. I know it's hard, but there's a protocol to follow, and I need to follow it. Sarah," she added, turning to face the girl, "You'll be in good hands, I promise. We'll help you, we're here for you."

Sarah was shaking her head, clinging to Tom and Mary, her eyes huge, her face chalk white. Jason stared at Winters. What was she? 22-23, just out of uni, a degree and student debts and fuck all knowledge about the real world. He tried to calm down. "Okay, look," he said, with an effort. "I'll try to keep it civil. Let's have a coffee, talk it through like grownups. Okay? Judith?" With a glance at the detective, who nodded, Judith agreed.

Chapter 15

"Sorry if we were rude," said Jason, as the adults sat around the kitchen table, coffee mugs steaming in front of them. "It's just... Sarah's such a lovely girl. All we want to do is help her. She's the most important person in this mess. I just can't get my head around what's happened, it's... bizarre."

Jason ran his hands down his face. He'd sensed tension between Lisa and George, but never expected anything like this. "You have to understand," said Judith. "We need to do what's best for the child. She'll be checked out and assessed by a therapist, taken into care where she can be safely looked after until we can agree on her long-term future. That's basically how the system works."

Back in the lounge, Tom was forming a plan. No way could he lose Sarah. Not while he was still breathing. Sarah was deeply upset and frightened. He took both her hands, turned her to face him. "Sarah, do you trust me?" he said.

"Yes, Tom. With my life."

"This is important. You have to pretend you can't lip read."

Sarah nodded, puzzled but willing to follow Tom's plan. Together, they walked into the kitchen. "Hi, Sarah," said Judith, getting up from the table. "I'm sorry this is happening. Are you ready to come with me?"

Tom stood beside Judith, repeating her words in sign. Judith looked at him in surprise. "Didn't you know?" he asked. "Sarah is deaf, confused and frightened to death. So unless you know sign language, I think it's best that I stay to interpret. Or you could write it all down, I suppose."

"Sorry, I didn't know," said Judith, suddenly less sure of herself. "I haven't had time to read Sarah's case notes."

"No problem," Tom said and signed. "Just speak slowly, and I'll keep up with you."

Judith started talking. Tom wasn't really listening, he was concentrating on his plan. "Sarah, I'm not going to let this woman take you away. This is your home now. We need to tell her you want to stay. Nod if you understand."

Sarah nodded, tears rolling down her face. The reality of the situation was hitting her hard. She should have stayed at the farm, looked after Lisa and shot that bastard George herself. "Okay," Tom went on. "Here's what I want you to do. Jump up and grab my mum. Scream and shout – 'Don't let them take me away, please, I love it here, please stop them, please help me.' Got it?"

Tom stepped back as Sarah raced over to Mary's chair, watching the social services woman. Would she have a heart and gave a fuck, or was she just another robot working for an inhumane system? He was pretty sure she could do something to let Sarah stay where she belonged. Sarah played her part well. But when he clocked Judith, he knew they were in deep trouble. A look of resignation was plastered across her face. A look that said it all. *This was going to be a difficult extraction.*

Judith sighed and phoned her boss, knowing that at this late hour and in the holidays he'd be as pissed off as she was. She couldn't get emotionally involved, she told herself. Her boss was no help at all, shouting at her to sort it out, like she had a magic wand, like she could fix it at the drop of a hat. All she knew, all she ever heard, was *'It doesn't work like that, it doesn't work like that.'*

Meantime, Mary was trying to comfort Sarah. Tom was glaring at Judith. Collins was being no help. And Jason was on the phone to his solicitor.

Chapter 16

Judith slammed her phone back in her bag and started to weep. She realised it was time, right now, to flip the coin, to get emotionally involved. To help Sarah. That poor girl, she'd be dumped in a kids' home on her own, not able to understand anyone. Grieving for her adoptive dad and worried about her mum being locked up. She'd be totally lost.

After a long, long pause, she looked at Tom. "Sod the bloody system," she said. "I know what's best for Sarah. I'm leaving her right here." Looking round at their surprised faces, she smiled ruefully. "I'm not heartless, you know," she said. "But that's not a long-term decision. You'll have to go through all the proper processes if you want to keep her for good. I can state my case, and I will, but you'll have to go through the system. The bloody, bloody system." She started to cry again. Tom felt for her. He paused, choosing his words carefully.

"It's the right call, Judith," he said, gently. "Sarah's had enough of a difficult life. She came to us with holes in her shoes and a threadbare coat — George Miller was a nasty piece of work, didn't care about her or Lisa. She'll be loved and looked after here. It's simple. We love her. We want her to stay. Take it from me, this is a happy home. I wake up every day and I feel blessed. Jason and Mary are amazing parents. So please, put that in your report. I love living here and so will Sarah. That's the truth."

Judith smiled. "I wish I had a friend like you, Tom," she said.

"Wish granted," said Tom. "You have a new friend."

Judith smiled. Tom smiled. All was good.

Turning to Mary and Jason, Judith said: "That's a bright young man, a credit to you both. I'm going to do what he would do. I'm going to fight tooth and nail for you, and for Sarah."

Jason nodded. "I've already spoken to my solicitor, we'll get the official wheels in motion as soon as possible," he said. "Mary and I would love to have Sarah living with us. She needs us right now — and we need her."

Judith brushed the hair out of her eyes and straightened up. "It's been a real pleasure meeting you all," she said. "I really think you've changed my life. I have to go now, but I'll pop by tomorrow to have a chat with Sarah. If that's okay with you?"

Mary shook Judith's hand. "Thank you, Judith," she said. "You'll be welcome."

Tom and Sarah watched from his bedroom window as Judith drove away. They sat on the bed, phones in hands. Tom was first to text.

Sorry about today.

I'm sorry about Lisa. I'm not sorry about George. I'm glad Lisa shot him. I'm just sad she's been arrested. She tried her best for me.

I hope you'll be allowed to live here now. I thought Judith was going to take you away for a minute there.

Me too. I really want to live here with you. I love Jason and Mary.

Dad's already phoned his solicitor, so we're on.

Thanks, Tom. I don't know what I'd do without you. I'm so glad you didn't die.

Yeah – me too!

They both laughed. Mary popped her head around the door. "I know it's late," she said, "But I'm making some bacon rolls. We all need something to eat."

Sarah jumped into Mary's arms. "Great!" she said. "But, please — no more marshmallows."

"No marshmallows, I promise," smiled Mary. "I'll give you a shout when the food's ready."

Outside, shivering in her patrol car, Susan Collins glanced at her watch. Her replacements should be here soon. With all the evidence she'd seen, she couldn't understand why Lisa had bothered to murder her husband.. He'd have rotted in prison for the rest of his life. Susan sighed. She had bigger problems. She was behind with her rent, and payday wasn't for another two weeks. She was slim, but unfit. Smoked too much, drank too much coffee. She mostly ate fast food, and her days off were usually spent drunk. She used to turn heads with her pretty face and smile, her tanned and toned legs under short skirts. Guys used to make a beeline for her. Not anymore. It was the stress of this job. She needed out. And for that, she needed money, and fast. If she didn't do it someone else would. She made a call to an ex-boyfriend, a news reporter. She hated the press, but needs must. He was a good looking guy and not bad in bed, maybe they might even try dating again. She was giving him a massive story, first bite of the cherry. Once the story hit the news channels, Oak Tree Farm and the local cop shop would be under siege.

Downstairs, Jason was watching the late news. It was not good news, even worse than he'd thought. A live report was coming from Oak Tree Farm. Mary quietly stepped into the room and watched with him. "Should we tell the kids about this?" she said, as she watched. Jason shook his head, switched off the TV. "Not tonight," he said. "I think we've all had enough bad news for one day."

Chapter 17

Monday. 30th December. 1 am.

Three cars pulled into the Drakes' drive. "At last," thought Collins, now she could go back to the police station and clock off. She might even crack open a bottle of wine when she got home, to celebrate her newfound wealth. A quick chat with the man in charge, then off she went, job done.

Tom saw the flashing lights through the blinds. What now? He looked out of the window as six armed officers got out of the cars and circled the house. He watched a man and a woman walk towards the front door. The loud knocking echoed throughout the house, sending shock waves through Tom's mind. Lights on, Tom followed his dad downstairs. Jason looked at Tom and opened the front door.

"Do you know what time it is?" he demanded. Detective Inspectors Chris Stevens and Wendy Curtis showed their ID. They were from New Scotland Yard — serious crime squad. "Sorry to wake you, Mr. Drake," said Stevens. "Please don't be alarmed. The armed officers are a precautionary measure. Can we come inside? It's a matter of utmost importance."

Jason let them in and led them through to the kitchen. "Okay Mr Drake," said Stevens. "We have to take immediate action. Sarah Miller could be in grave danger. She needs to be placed under police protection. The information we have from Lisa Miller tells us a dangerous assassin is on the loose, hired by George Miller to kill the Prime Minister."

Jason nodded wearily, as Tom kept a poker face. "I watched the news," said Jason. "I still can't get my head around it. Sarah's sleeping, do you have to take her away now? Can't you come back later? The poor child has been through so much."

"I'm afraid so, sir," said Stevens, sounding almost as tired as he looked. At 46 years old, he looked much older, stress had aged him. He was short and stocky, with grey, receding short hair, bushy eyebrows, and bags under his bloodshot eyes. His suit was creased and his shoes were covered in mud. He looked a tired old man. But something told Tom not to underestimate him. This was a good, experienced copper. His colleague had said nothing so far, just eyeballed Tom and Jason with a keen, bright gaze.

"Sorry, sir," Stevens went on. "We are dealing with a very dangerous situation here."

"This is mad," said Tom, keeping his frayed nerves under control. "Do you really believe anyone in their right mind would try to assassinate the PM? Sounds a bit far-fetched..."

"Believe me," said Stevens. "I wish it was. But it's a fact — the PM and Sarah are both potentially in great danger.

Mary came downstairs. Tom noticed she had her bed socks on. At least her feet wouldn't get cold. "What on earth is going on?" she asked.

"You'd better sit down," said Jason, looking at his wife. "It's not good news. This is Chris and Wendy from the serious crime squad. The TV news was spot on, an assassin is on the loose. They're worried that Sarah might be a target."

"Oh my word," said Mary, sitting down, visibly shocked. "So what happens now?"

They sat in silence for a few minutes. "Okay," said Stevens. "Full disclosure. What we know is that George hired a highly-skilled assassin. He's top of the most wanted list in Europe and the USA. The media have nicknamed him The Eagle, because he always shoots his targets through the eye. Eagle-eye, see? It's the media," he added. "It doesn't have to make a lot of sense.

"Anyway, according to Lisa Miller, the hit is set for tomorrow night, after the countdown to the New Year and just as the PM sets off the fireworks at the London Eye. It's a serious threat. We can't afford to ignore it."

A shiver ran down Tom's spine. The Eagle was dead. He'd had a massive heart attack on his 40th birthday. This wasn't possible — unless someone else had adopted the name... He fought to stay calm, to make sense of the situation.

"Wait a minute," said Jason. "If you know so much about this threat, why don't you just stop the PM from being there? Surely that makes sense? Why would he put himself at risk?"

Chris and Wendy rolled their eyes. "I — ahem — I wish it was that simple, sir," said Stevens. The unspoken words hovered in the air: *bloody stubborn politicians. Strangers to common sense. Or any sense at all.*

"Look, can you get Sarah ready to travel?" said Stevens. "The sooner she's out of here the better. She'll be safe. Once we catch the assassin she'll come back. But I can't guarantee her safety if she stays here. It's too open to attack."

"Thanks, Mrs Drake," said Stevens. "DI Curtis here will follow you up, keep an eye on the grounds from upstairs. Can't be too careful."

Wendy didn't say a word, just slipped off her shoes and followed Mary upstairs.

"Do you know Sarah is deaf?" asked Tom, while they waited. "Can you sign?"

"Yes Tom," Stevens replied. "I can't sign but we have pads and pens ready, so communication won't be a problem. Judith said you can sign — how about you interpret for me while I introduce myself to Sarah? I'd appreciate it."

"Sure, sir," said Tom, playing the helpful schoolboy card to the hilt. "Happy to help! You seem like one of the good guys — like James Bond: 007, licensed to kill. Do you have a contact card? Will I be able to keep in touch with Sarah?"

Stevens smiled and handed a card to Tom. He wished he was a movie star. "You'll be able to contact Sarah," he said. "But only for a limited time each day. We have to monitor who she has contact with for her own safety. She'll be in a safe house, protected 24/7. I'll let you know the best times to text her."

Tom nodded. Mary, Sarah, and Wendy came down, Sarah holding Mary's hand, looking sleepy and scared. Tom looked at Sarah. "The copper wants a word," he signed. "He's a good guy, he just wants to protect you. I'll sign for him, okay?"

Sarah nodded. Tom's heart went out to her. He nodded to Stevens.

Chris spoke quietly, reassuringly. Tom signed his own version of the words. "Sarah, you need to go with them — it's just for a little while. They'll take you to a safe house, you'll be in no danger from anyone, whatever they say. I'll miss you, but we'll text every day, let us agree a time, say 8 pm, and as soon as they catch this assassin, you'll be able to come home for good. Please try to stay positive— think of this like an adventure, and remember that I love you."

"Okay Tom," signed Sarah, although tears were running down her face. "I trust you. I'll go with them. I love you too."

"We'll get you home, where you belong, as soon as possible," signed Tom. "We'll be together always."

Sarah nodded miserably. Just when things were looking up, it had all gone crazy again. It might only be temporary, but it wasn't going to be easy. She had to stay strong. She hugged Jason and Mary, saying. "Thank you both so much, for everything. Look after each other while I'm away. I love you both."

The coppers were waiting by the door, Stevens speaking into his handset, telling his men to get ready. Sarah kissed Tom's cheek. "I love you," she signed.

"I'll see you soon, Sarah, I promise," he replied.

Tom stood between his mum and dad, watching as Sarah and the police officers got in the cars. Tom waved and tried to smile. The three cars started to reverse out of the driveway. Tom turned and raced up the stairs. He picked up his phone and sent a text.

I love you, Sarah Miller.

There was a buzz — Sarah's phone was on his bed. No way. Panic-stricken, he grabbed it, ripped the charger from the socket and bounded down the stairs. He bolted out of the front door, still in slippers. No time to put his trainers on. "Sarah's left her phone behind," he yelled, as he sprinted across the snow-covered drive.

"Run like the wind, Tom!" Mary shouted after him. "Run like the wind!"

The police cars were 200m ahead, slowly making their way up the snowy hill. His mothers' words — both his mother's — echoing through his mind: *run like the wind*. Behind him, Jason grabbed his coat and went after him.

Tom sprinted faster. If the lights weren't red at the crossroads, he'd lose his chance. He was running flat out. The hill was steep, his lungs were on fire. He reached the crest of the hill. The cars were only another 100m ahead, stopped at the lights. His legs worked harder than ever before, his arms slashed through the air. Catching up with the convoy, he desperately bashed on the window. "Sarah!" he shouted, as she turned, startled. "Sarah, your phone!" Stevens opened the window and took the phone and charger from the exhausted boy. Curtis was just looking at him in astonishment. If he'd had the breath, Tom would have laughed at her expression. Sarah twisted around, trying to grab a last glimpse as the traffic lights changed and the convoy drove away.

Tom's chest, legs, feet, and lungs hurt, his shirt was soaked with sweat. His legs were like jelly, his heart was pumping dangerously and he was fighting for air. He'd just sprinted 300m uphill and another hundred on the flat. He collapsed onto the pavement. He tried to get up, but his body was empty. His muscles cramped, the pain was intense. He felt weak, almost frozen in time.

Jason reached his boy, gently helped him to stand and wrapped a coat around him, held his arm to help him home. "Thanks, Dad," Tom managed. "I'd have struggled without you."

Back in the house, Jason helped Tom upstairs, while Mary ran a hot bath. Jason helped his son in, then fetched a mop and bucket to clean the mud off the kitchen and hall floors.

Tom lay back, already feeling better. After a 15-minute soak, he got out and managed — stiffly, to get into his pyjamas. He was exhausted

— it was time for bed. He shuffled onto his bed, eased himself back onto the pillows, and picked up his phone to see a text from Sarah.

Are you okay?? I saw you collapse. They wouldn't stop the car. I'm so angry with them. I'm going out of my mind.

He replied, pronto.

I'm fine, Sarah – was just in the bath. Haven't run like that in my life before! Needed to soak my legs. Are you okay? Text me tonight at 8 pm. Love you.

Mary came in with a hot chocolate drink. "No more action hero stuff tonight, Tom," she said, only half-joking. "I need to relax and get some sleep."

"I promise, Mum," he said, trying to smile. "Thanks for this. I'm not going to have any trouble sleeping tonight — I'm right out of energy. Would you believe it?"

Chapter 18

30th December.

No-one moved in the house next morning til after 10am — everyone was exhausted from the adventurous night before. Tom, as usual, was first up, and got straight onto his laptop for some serious research. Time was tight. He had to assess how recent events had affected his plans.

Breakfast was more of a brunch today, but before they'd finished they were interrupted by a loud knocking at the front door. "I'll go," said Jason, with a smile on his face. "I wonder if it's one of the neighbours. This used to be such a quiet street." He was still smiling as he opened the door. A smile that quickly vanished.

"Good morning, Mr Drake," said a stranger on the doorstep, rudely pushing the door wider. "I'm Colin Stiles from The Daily Horizon. Can I come in? I'd like your story on the recent events. It'll only take a few minutes, and my editor's willing to pay for an exclusive."

Colin had made a huge mistake. He'd stepped right over the door, putting his snowy, muddy shoe right on the clean hall floor. Jason was a calm, easy-going sort of guy, and it took a lot to make him angry. But between yesterday and this, he'd been pushed far enough. He placed a mighty hand in the middle of Colin Stiles' chest, and shoved. It caught the reporter by surprise, and he keeled over, flat on his back in the snow.

"Not today, thanks," Jason spat. "Get off my property or I'll call the police. Don't even think about coming back."

He slammed the door and shook his head. But he'd sent a message to Stiles and to the other reporters he'd spotted lurking beyond the hedge. *Stay away from my family.* He went back to the kitchen, muttering to himself, but had barely picked up his coffee mug when the doorbell chimed.

He sprang into action mode, now he would give that reporter a right hook. He wrenched open the door, fist at the ready. To his surprise, it was Judith Winters. The scruffy reporter was slowly walking away.

"Oh! Morning Judith," he said, hastily dropping his hand. "Come on in. There's coffee ready. Let me take your coat." He escorted Judith into the kitchen. Tom smiled. Judith had considerately taken her shoes off and left them on the porch.

"Hello Judith," said Mary. "Coffee?"

"Yes please," said Judith, gratefully. "Hi Mary, hi Tom."

"Good to see you," said Tom. "Any news?"

"Yes Tom, some good news, I think. I wrote my report and gave it to my boss — and your dad's solicitor phoned him at 9 am this morning. Put the fear of God into him. So I'm pretty confident that Sarah will be back with you as soon as it's safe for her. Poor kid. She must be so confused. I'm pretty confused myself. Oh — before I forget: Lisa Miller hasn't been charged yet."

"That all sounds really positive, Judith, thank you," said Mary. Jason nodded his agreement, handing out biscuits with a wide grin. Tom felt happier too, especially since he knew Sarah wasn't in any danger. At least, he didn't see how she could be.

"I have to go," said Judith, eventually. "I just want to thank all of you again. Being with you, seeing who you are, has made me realise what's important. Before now, I'd thought about packing in my job. But I won't. I'm going to stay and try to make the system better. I'm going to help as many people as I can."

With that, she sailed blithely out of the kitchen, a new, invigorated woman. This was the happiest she'd ever been. "Come and see us anytime," Tom called from the front door, as she got into her car. "You'll always be welcome here!"

And Judith thought she just might.

Chapter 19

Tom knew Sarah would be safe. Even if there was somehow another Eagle, another him out there, there's no way Sarah would have seen him. No way on earth he'd ever have met his client. But he had no choice but to go along with it. It was time to share his plan.

"Mum, Dad, I want to talk to you both," he said, going back into the kitchen. They looked up, surprised at the serious tone in his voice. "Please just hear me out before you say anything," he added. "Here it is: we need this assassin to be caught before Sarah can come home. I think the police will need help doing that. And I believe I can give it to them."

Mary had her hands over her mouth. Jason was about to speak. "Please dad, let me finish," said Tom. "I know this sounds mad, but I also know it's something I need to do. The police have been hunting this man for 20 years. We need to flip the coin, make the hunter into the hunted. And I have a plan..."

"No way!" said Mary, jumping up, unable to contain herself any longer. "Are you out of your mind? Just let the police do their job, Tom, and I'll do mine — which is keeping you out of harm's way! Jason, talk to him, please. Make him see sense. Talk him out of whatever it is he thinks he's going to do."

Tom held his hand up again, desperate to get his message across. "Please, guys, please just listen. I've done my homework. This Eagle disappeared off the radar about five years ago. There's been nothing seen or heard of him in all that time. So he's rusty. And he's getting old. I'm betting this is one last big payday to fund his retirement. And I'm betting I know how to stop him."

"How?" said Jason, in spite of himself. Mary gasped and held her hands up high. "Jason, no way!" she yelped. "You can't be serious! What on earth has got into you? I mean, I want to help Sarah as much as either of you do, but this is crazy! It won't work, because I'm not letting it happen! Do I make myself clear?"

"Look," said Jason, "I'm just interested to hear Tom's plan. I'm not making any decisions. There can't be any harm in just hearing a plan, can there?"

"What does it matter what the plan is?" spluttered Mary. "We can't possibly agree to it! It's far too dangerous! My God, this is just madness!"

Tom sat quiet, giving Mary time to calm down a little. When she'd run out of words, he spoke again. "Listen, Mum, please," he said. "It's really simple, and the key is Dad's penthouse apartment. It's the perfect location to see and not be seen. We need to be there on New Year's Eve, and keep a lookout for the Eagle."

"Okay," said Mary, hands on her hips. "And then what? How do you plan to stop him?"

"We don't," said Tom. "We just spot him, tell Chris Stevens and let the cops take over. Honest. There's no way I'd put you or dad in any danger. This is just about being an extra pair of eyes." He held his breath. Would she go for it? He knew his plan would put only one person in danger — himself. But he couldn't tell them that. This was the only way. He breathed out as Mary sat back in her chair, looking at her husband.

"I mean, what could happen?" said Jason. "There's no way anyone else can get into that building, and we'd be right out of reach of any trouble. Look. Tom just wants to feel like he's helping Sarah. I think we can help him do that, don't you?" Mary looked doubtful.

"You're not going to try to do anything... stupid?" she said, warily. "No action-hero stuff?"

"No, Mum," said Tom, mentally crossing his fingers behind his back. "Just watching and calling the cops."

Mary sighed. "I'll think about it," she said, and Tom knew the battle was won. As long as Mary thought she was only humouring him, everything was going according to plan. The next step was a reconnaissance mission. Tom persuaded her that he and Jason should go to the apartment that afternoon. "I'm still not promising anything, mind," she said. Tom grinned.

After lunch, Jason drove Tom to the apartment building in London. They went straight to the top floor. Tom surveyed the view from the balcony, overlooking the Thames. Binoculars out, he scanned the buildings across the river, inch by inch.

His mind was focused on where the assassin would be. Where would he have gone? Which building? And why? The penthouse was the perfect location to get a clear shot at the PM, and it might be the right spot to reach the assassin. George must have hired two, he realised. Typical of the man. Spend a fortune on bloody assassins while his wife and daughter froze and starved in that mouldy old dump of a house.

Back to the matter in hand. The assassin would likely be on the other side of the river. It was only an educated guess, but it felt right. Jason and Tom strolled across Westminster Bridge to get a better view of the buildings. Tom noticed they were higher on this side.

Let's see... there would be police marksmen on quite a few buildings, the more obvious ones at least. And he'd need to be able to get to ground cover as quickly as possible afterwards, lose himself in the crowd.

Tom glanced at the London Eye as they crossed the bridge again and went back up to the penthouse. He looked at the buildings again, and suddenly it hit him. He knew where the assassin would be. It was like a great big neon finger was pointing at it. He nudged Jason. "There," he said. "Do you see it? The Tower crane."

Chapter 20

"That's it, dad, I know it. It's the highest point, the perfect view. But it's not somewhere the police will cover – they'll be looking at buildings."

Jason nodded. "Alright, son, so far so good," he said. "So, tell me, what's your plan? Not the one you told your mother. Your real plan. How are you going to stop him?"

"I'm going to shoot him," said Tom, simply. No point denying it. If Jason had worked it out and was still here, he was already on side. "I'll wound him, then let the police take over. You and me will stay here. Mum doesn't need to be involved. What do you say?"

"I'm going to watch your back like a bloody hawk, is what I say," answered Jason. "I hope your plan works, young man, or we're in big trouble. Cause your mum'll kill us both. One question – what're you going to shoot him with? Your rifle isn't powerful enough."

"We have a rifle," said Tom, lowering his gaze to the floor. "It's on top of the elevator. George Miller put it there after he tried to hire me to shoot the PM."

Jason suddenly sat on a wooden crate. "What the — what was George thinking?" he spluttered. "I knew he wanted something from us, but I didn't see this coming. That bastard — if I'd known about this, I'd have shot him myself. Why didn't you tell me, son? Why didn't you mention it to the detective?"

Tom laughed. "Imagine me coming home and saying 'Hi Dad, how's things? By the way, George Miller asked me to assassinate the PM.' I couldn't tell you, the detective, anyone. They'd have thought I was making it up. I'm still not sure how I'm going to tell mum. She'll hit the bloody roof."

"Language," said Jason, automatically, then laughed. "I guess you're right," he said. "I wouldn't have believed you. Jesus. Alright, let's find this rifle, if it's there, get it safely stashed."

"Thanks, Dad," said Tom. "First things first, eh?"

"One other question," said Jason, as they made their way to the elevator shaft. "What about this other assassin George apparently hired? Why did he try to hire you as well?"

"Back-up, I think," said Tom, shrugging. "He'd seen me shoot. He probably thought I'd be a cheap Plan B."

At the elevator, Jason stood on a step ladder and opened the service hatch. Tom hauled himself up and retrieved the weapon, wrapped in a blanket. Tom laid it on the floor and unrolled it. A Russian-made Kalashnikov SVCH-308, infra-red telescopic sights, with an effective shooting range of around 1000m and a built-in barrel tripod for stability.

They stood in silence for a few minutes, the reality of the situation hitting home. A wave of emotion hit Tom. He'd used a rifle like this before, in his previous life. The face of the man he'd assassinated flashed through his mind. He felt dizzy, sat down on the floor, breathing slow. He had to stay calm, or he'd lose this chance to do the job he was sent back to do.

Jason finally spoke. He looked like a deflated balloon. "Jesus Christ," he croaked. "We have to tell the police about this, son. George must have been mixed up with some seriously dangerous people to get hold of this weapon. I'm concerned for our safety — for your safety. Whoever hid this rifle knows we're involved, and we don't know who that is. This is way out of our league. I'm sorry, Tom. It's just too risky. It stops now."

Tom nodded. "I understand, Dad," he said. "But think about this. Would George be likely to tell anyone he'd hired a 15-year-old boy? Especially if they're as dangerous as you say. They'd have shot him on the spot. So honestly, I don't think anyone will have made the link between this building and you or me. It's just a building George was involved in. He's the reason everything's been going wrong, by the way. He's been sabotaging you for months."

"Bastard!" spat Jason. "I bloody knew it!" He looked at his son, still not completely convinced.

"Look, Dad," said Tom. "The only way I can stop all this is to take out the assassin. It's ironic, really. George tried to hire me as back up, and now I'm going to stop the whole plan, using the rifle he supplied. We tell the police, we lose the weapon. And I can't stop the Eagle without it. You know I can do this, Dad. You've seen me shoot. I have a chance to save a life here. If you had that chance, I know you wouldn't walk away from it. I'm 100% sure of it." Jason stared at Tom. For a few seconds, time stood still. Then the big man knelt on the floor, and wrapped the rifle back in the blanket.

"You're right," he said. "I wouldn't." he sighed. "Let's go home, son," he said, putting the rifle back on top of the elevator. "I just don't know how in hell I'm going to explain all this to your mother."

Mary opened the door to greet them as they pulled back into the driveway. "I'm glad you're home," she said. "I was worried. I've made a stew. Let's have a nice family meal, and you can tell me all about your afternoon." Her face was pinched with worry, but she tried to smile.

After supper, Tom left Jason wondering how to break the news to Mary, and went upstairs to finalise his plan. He downloaded and printed a Google Earth map, used it to calculate distance and angles. He checked the weather forecast for the following night. High winds or heavy rain would impact his shot. He believed the assassin's plan was to shoot the PM, abseil down the crane and make his getaway among the crowds. Happy New Year.

Plan complete, Tom wrote a letter to DI Stevens, explaining everything as well as he could. He sealed it in an envelope. He'd give it to his mum to look after, in case anything went wrong at the penthouse. Next, his thoughts turned to Sarah. It was time for their nightly chat. Right on cue, his phone buzzed.

Hi Tom. How are you? I'm missing you.

I'm fine Sarah. In fact, I'm great — Judith came to see us today. She says there's a good chance you'll be able to live with us permanently.

That's fantastic! Oh, that's cheered me up so much. I want so much to be with you.

Ditto. Believe me, we'll make this happen. Are they treating you well?

Yes. But I'm lonely at night. And I'm worried about Lisa. Have you heard anything? I only know she hasn't been charged.

Lisa is helping the police. No, she hasn't been charged yet. She's a brave lady, Sarah. I'm sure she'll be okay.

Thanks, Tom, I hope you're right. I'll say a prayer for her. Give my love to Jason and Mary, okay? I have to go now. I'll message you tomorrow, same time. Love you. x

Goodnight Sarah. I love you too.

Sarah went to her room, sat on the bed and picked up her diary.

Dear Mum. It's days like this I miss you the most. You were so young when you died. I came home from school and there you were on the floor. You felt so cold. I got a blanket and put it over you, then phoned 999. I tried to get you into the recovery position, like you told me to do when someone isn't well, but you were too heavy for me to move. I don't think it would have made any difference. I miss your hugs. I miss you telling me everything will be okay. I miss you brushing my hair, and kissing me goodnight. I miss your smile. But that's the sad part of my letter out of the way. I did like you said I should, all those years ago. I found someone who makes me smile. His name is Tom. He is my pot of gold at the end of the rainbow. The sun always shines when I'm with him. He loves me, and makes me happy. And I love him with all my heart. I know he's the one, Mum, I feel so lonely and empty when I'm not with him. His parents are wonderful too. They're so kind, so warm. Their house is a home. I'm going to live with them soon. So you don't need to worry about me, Mum. I hope you're as happy in heaven as I will be when I'm with Tom forever. I love you, always.

Mary came upstairs to find Tom with his hand on his heart, eyes closed. He opened them and smiled at his mum as she sat on his bed. She looked worried. There were lines round her eyes he'd never seen before. "I'm sorry to cause you so much stress," he said.

"Sshh," she answered. "It can't be helped. Your dad and I have had a long chat. I'm not happy, Tom. But when it comes down to saving a life or walking away, how can I say no? But I'm warning you," she threatened. "If anything happens to you or your dad, I'll bloody murder you myself."

She stroked Tom's hair. "You look tired," she said. "You need a good night's sleep. How's Sarah? Are they treating her well?"

"She's good, mum," he said, closing his eyes. "She sends her love. I'm missing her, you know?" He yawned, hugely. "Night mum," he mumbled. "I love you."

"Sleep well, Tom," said Mary, softly. "I love you too. So very much."

She turned the light out and closed the door, leaning against it for a moment with tears meeting on her chin. She was terrified. How could this be happening? "Please God," she whispered. "Please — keep him safe."

Elsewhere, as Tom drifted into sleep, a tall, well-dressed man got off the train from Glasgow.

Chapter 21

31st December. New Year's Eve.

6 am. Tom was in the kitchen, drinking coffee. Everything hinged on today. They'd all go to London early, go sight-seeing to blend in. Just like the killer would be doing. Getting a feel for the area, the killing zone. It was going to be a long day.

He waited until 7am, then made breakfast. A tray of bacon and tomato rolls, and more coffee. He took the breakfast up to his mum and dad, feeling nervous as he knocked on the door. What if they'd changed their minds? But the fact that he wasn't locked in his room seemed like a good start.

"Morning!" he said, brightly. "Breakfast is served!"

"What's this in aid of?" asked Mary.

"Well, I just think we should head into London early today," he said. "It's going to get busy later on, and we need time to check some things out. Sorry, I sound so bossy. I'm just trying to plan out the day as closely as I can."

"It's fine Tom," said Jason, grabbing a roll. "Have you checked the train times?"

"You know me, Dad," grinned Tom. "There's a direct train at 8.47 am, so eat up! And I've grilled those tomatoes, just the way you like them."

A little over an hour later, they were on the fast train from Richmond to Waterloo. Tom gave Mary and Jason a brief description of the Eagle. "So we're looking for a tall man, somewhere around 45 – 50, fair hair, slim but strong. Blue eyes. He's thought to be Scottish, but no-one can confirm that. And remember, he's dangerous. If you even think you've spotted him, play it cool.

"I think we'll start on the south of the river," he went on. "We just want to get an idea of how it's all going to play out this evening, where the PM will be, where the crowds will be. That's our focus, not spotting this guy.

I'd like you to go home at four, Mum, please. I need you to give the letter I've left in the kitchen to DI Stevens. Don't worry mum, it's just a safeguard if we get arrested. It explains all about my plan."

Mary looked miserable. "I'm not happy about leaving you," she said.

"I know Mum," said Tom, "But please, trust me. I know what I'm doing — it's all planned out. And Dad'll be with me to watch my back."

Jason was in quiet mode. He was extremely worried. He was pleased Mary had agreed to Tom's plan — at least she'd be out of harm's way. Fear, wonder, horror and disbelief washed over him by turns. All he could do was watch Tom's back and hope.

They spent an hour walking on the south side of the river, then crossed Westminster Bridge. Mary took loads of photos. They even got a friendly woman to take some snaps of the three of them for the family album. Tom did a few sketches. Jason kept a watchful eye.

Sitting huddled together on a bench to have lunch, Tom stared across the river at the giant crane and bit his lip. At midnight he would have to regress to his previous life. He'd have to shoot another human being. He had a bad feeling, mostly sadness. But there was no point looking back. This was all about moving forward.

"He's close," he said, half to himself. "I can feel it. Dad, let's get mum to the station, then we need to head back to the penthouse."

Tom stood, dropping their sandwich wrappers into a nearby bin, idly watching an old man in an electric wheelchair head towards them. "Good to see a young man disposing of rubbish properly," the old man smiled, as he got close. His legs were covered in a heavy blue blanket, and he wore a bobble hat, gloves, and a thick red scarf. A grey, Santa-type beard framed a nondescript, heavily-lined, suntanned face. He showed yellow, stained teeth as he smiled at Tom.

"What's your name, son?" he asked, his voice vaguely American. "I'm Thomas Drake, sir," Tom replied. My friends call me Tom."

"I bet you have lots of friends, a good looking guy like you," said the old man.

"No sir, just one. Her name's Sarah."

"That's one more than me since my wife passed away," the old man sighed. "She used to love watching the New Year fireworks. Will you be watching them here, or in the warm on TV?"

"We're going to watch them live. We'll think of your wife, enjoying them from heaven," said Tom.

"That's nice, son, thank you," said the man. "It's real nice to meet a polite young man like you. I'll be on my way now. Cold weather, you see? Plays havoc with my old bones. Goodbye, Tom."

"Goodbye, sir."

Tom watched the old man drop his empty coffee cup in the bin, reverse his chair and go on his way. He raised his left hand. "Enjoy the fireworks!" he called, out as he weaved his way through the pedestrians.

Tom smiled and waved back. He turned to his parents. "What a nice old boy," he said.

Chapter 22

Jason and Tom walked back to the penthouse. Tom was on the balcony with his dad's binoculars, scanning the walkways and tall buildings when something hit him like a giant demolition ball. He'd just made a huge mistake. He was only human, after all. He grabbed his sketchbook and drew exactly what had caught his attention, then showed it to his dad.

"Bloody hell's bells," said Jason, looking at the drawing of the old man. The arms of the wheelchair were shaped like two halves of a rifle butt. Because that is exactly what they were. The rest of the weapon must have been hidden in the chair. "What do we do now?" he said. "Search for him? Let the police know?"

"No point, Dad," said Tom. "He'll have changed his appearance by now. I messed up, didn't spot him. All we can do is stick to the plan and wait."

Tom sat on the floor and shut his eyes. He tried to meditate, to clear all negative thoughts from his overactive mind. A four-letter word kept running through his brain: fear. He was terrified for Jason, Mary, and Sarah. Jason interrupted him with a tap on the shoulder. He opened his eyes. His dad handed him his phone. "Your mum," he said.

"Hi Mum," said Tom. "I'm glad to know you're safe."

"How are you feeling?" asked Mary. "Are you okay?"

"I'm good thanks, mum, ready for action. Thunderbirds are go!"

"Tom, please be careful," she said. "This isn't a game. Promise me you'll let the police know as soon as you spot the assassin."

"I promise, Mum," he fibbed. "It'll all work out, you'll see. What are you going to do while we wait?"

"I'm going to be glued to the fireworks on the bloody TV," said Mary, in tones of steel. "Stay safe, son. I love you."

His dad was looking really stressed as he hung up the phone. "I'm on edge," he said.

"Me too, Dad," said Tom. "We'd be fools if we weren't. This is serious stuff. We're only human, you know?"

Jason nodded. "You're right, son," he said. "You know, when this is all over, I think we should go fishing. Just the two of us. Mum detests sitting on a riverbank. I think it's calming. Peaceful. Relaxing. Can't think of a better way to de-stress."

"Sounds great, Dad," said Tom. "What's the biggest fish you've ever caught? A shark? A whale? Maybe a jellyfish?"

They both smiled. The idle chat was helping. "I've never caught a fish in my life," Jason replied. "I'm the worst fisherman who ever lived. I just liked going out with my dad. We used to sit for hours, just taking in nature at its best. I loved it. I miss my old dad, you know? And my mum. They'd have loved you."

"I bet they were great," said Tom. "You can tell me all about them, when we're sitting on the riverbank, not catching any fish."

For the rest of the evening, as the sky grew ever darker, they took turns out on the balcony, monitoring the crane and the river. By 7.30pm, they could see police marksmen taking up positions on the buildings around the Eye, but no sign of the assassin. This concerned Tom. If a marksman spotted him with a rifle in his hands, he'd be dead. And fair enough — the police had a job to do.

8 pm. They went back inside away from prying eyes. Sitting by the front door, they ate the rest of the food and drink they'd brought. Jason fired up a gas heater, carefully positioned away from the windows so the light wouldn't give them away. Tom got the rifle and checked the ammo for the thousandth time. He jumped about a mile when his phone buzzed in his pocket. Sarah.

Hi, Tom. You staying up to watch the fireworks?

Hey! Yeah, Dad and I are in London to watch them live. Are you staying up?

No — it won't be fun without you.

*Just think of next year, when we'll be watching them together.
And we'll have a mini-display in the back garden when you get home.*

Ha - yes, I'll look forward to that. You'd better make it a good one!

That's a promise, Sarah,

Thanks, Tom. Gotta go again. Have a great night. Love you.

Love you too, Sarah. Happy New Year when it comes.

Sarah shut off her phone and looked around the quiet, comfortable but dull little bedroom she was occupying. She was safe, but she was also bored, bored, bored. Grabbing a pen, she flipped her diary open.

Dear Lisa. I'm sorry I wasn't there for you when you needed me. I'm not angry you shot George. I hated the bastard. I just feel guilty that I went to stay with Tom and left you on your own. I wish you'd found as good a man as I have. I wish you'd left George. We'd have been okay, you and me. Now you're probably going to prison, and I'm really worried about you. How will you cope with prison life? You're not a criminal. You just did what you had to do. I'll come and visit you as soon as I can, and I'll be there for you when you get out. I was hoping the New Year would bring us all happiness, instead of all this stress. But I'm grateful to you, Lisa. I know you tried your best to look after me. I believe you knew Mary and Jason would open their hearts and give me a good home. I can't change what's happened, but I can change the future. I'm going to study, get my A levels, get a job and work hard, buy a house, so when you're free, you can live with us. Tom and me. He'll keep us safe, that's a promise.

Chapter 23

At 10 pm, Jason set up a trestle on the balcony, using two Black and Decker workbenches with three short planks laid across them. He put a blanket over the top, holding it down with clips. Now Tom had a hide. He crawled in, and Jason passed him the rifle. He lay down and got as comfortable as possible. Through his telescopic night-vision sights, he viewed every building across the river, ending up fully focused on the crane.

Jason checked the first aid box, just in case of an emergency. The crowds below were swelling, hundreds of happy people waiting to celebrate. According to the news, there wouldn't be any long-winded speeches — the PM was going to emerge just two minutes before he hit the button. Tom surveyed the barge he knew the man was waiting on, taking a mental note of where he'd be standing when he came out.

11 pm. Tom crawled out of his hide. "Dad, Chris Stevens' number is on my phone," he said. "I'll let you know as soon as I spot the Eagle. Then you call Stevens straight away and tell him where he is and where we are. Okay?"

"No problem, son," said Jason, firmly.

Tom handed over his phone and crawled back under the blanket. "Wish me luck, Dad," he said. "I really hope I've got this right.".

"Good luck, son," said Jason, and added to himself: "So do I, my boy. So do I."

11.30 pm. Still no movement on the crane.

11.45 pm. Nothing.

11.55 pm. Still nothing.

"Have I got this wrong?" thought Tom. "What if the assassin kills the PM? It'll be my fault — I missed him earlier..."

11.58 pm. The prime minister appeared on the barge, waving to the masses. Cheers — and boos — erupted. Tom focused on the crane, and slowly saw the end of a rifle appear.

"I've seen him!" he called. "He's on the crane, just below the cab! I – dammit, I can't get a clear shot. Phone Stevens', Dad, right now!"

As Jason made the call, sweat formed on Tom's brow, as the final minute began. He only needed one chance. Suddenly, he saw it. "Dad," he said, quietly. "Do you trust me?"

"Of course, son."

"I'm changing the plan," said Tom. "I just hope it works."

The crowd had started chanting. Ten, nine, eight, seven...

Tom knew he was about to take a huge gamble. He took aim.

Six, five, four...

He had no choice.

Three, two, O...! Tom fired as the first rockets went up, hoping he'd got it right.

The PM went down, as the bullet struck his head. His bodyguards dived to shield him, pulling his lifeless form undercover. Tom reloaded and flicked his attention back towards the crane. "Shit!" roared Jason. "The PM's been shot!"

"Get down, Dad!" screamed Tom. "It's not over yet! I shot him!"

Jason flung himself onto the floor. "What? WHAT?" he bellowed from the carpet. "What the FUCK is going on?"

"Language," muttered Tom, desperately focusing on the crane. He only had one more shot. He saw a shadow begin to move down the ladder beneath the cab. Light glinted for a second on a Karabiner. The Eagle was about to abseil from his nest. Tom drew a deep breath, and gently squeezed the trigger. The shot went right through the man's left shoulder.

Happy New Year.

At that exact moment, Tom felt an impact in his own left shoulder as a bullet embedded itself. The pain was excruciating. He dropped his head, giving in. He'd given it his best shot.

Tom didn't hear the apartment door being bashed open, or the armed police enter. He didn't hear his dad calling his name. He wasn't aware of being rushed to a waiting ambulance. He didn't see or hear the fireworks, or the shrill of the sirens. He swam in darkness, cold and numb, hanging on for dear life. Just like the Eagle, hanging onto the crane ladder, looking at the oblivious crowds swarming below.

Jason and DI Stevens were in the ambulance with the badly-injured Tom. They were heading for St George's University Hospital, the major trauma centre for knife and/or bullet wounds. It was about seven miles from the London Eye. Things were not looking good. Stevens' called Mary — Jason wouldn't take his hand off his son's wound, desperately trying to staunch the flow of blood. A police car was on its way to bring her to the hospital.

Chapter 24

Mary had never been so worried. What had she been thinking, agreeing to this mad plan? If only she could turn back time... She was frantic, her hands were shaking. She couldn't stop the tears. Who shot him? Who shot her son?

In the ambulance, Tom's heart stopped. The paramedic leapt into action, performing CPR. Jason kept pressure on the wadding over Tom's injury. "Don't die, Tom," he whispered. "Please, please don't die!"

The paramedic, Tracy Bryant, checked for a pulse. No luck. It wasn't the wound, or the blood loss. Tom's body was simply in shock. It just wanted to shut down. Tracy wasn't going to let it. She'd been saving lives for years. No way she was letting this boy die without a fight. She quickly fired up the defibrillator and picked up the pads.

"Clear!" she yelled. "Jason! Clear!"

Jason didn't move. He looked at Tracy. "I can't," he said. "Just do it. Just bloody do it." Tracy didn't argue. She sent a huge electric current through Tom's body. Jason didn't even feel it — his hand held firm. Tracy stared, goggle-eyed. But it had worked. Tom's pulse was back and his blood pressure was on the rise. "I can see where he gets his fighting spirit from," she said. "Well done. Keep the pressure on."

Detective Stevens was blasting out orders on his phone. "Get the roads cleared," he was yelling. "Do you hear me? Just get them fucking clear, and have a crash team waiting!"

"How long, Roy?" shouted Tracy to the driver.

"ETA five minutes!"

"Pedal to the metal Roy," Tracy called back. "Pedal to the metal."

Tom's heart stopped again. Fuck. Tracy knew this was her last throw, shit or bust. She pulled out the big, pre-loaded adrenaline needle and plunged it into his chest, injecting the stimulant into Tom's heart. "Come on, Tom!" she screamed. "Come on!"

Tom was floating, peaceful. He watched the paramedic and his dad battling to save him. It was almost over. He felt an inner calm as he got ready to meet his maker, whoever that was. He heard voices. His mum — his birth mum — calling his name. Suddenly he was in a garden, surrounded by beautiful flowers, a blue sky smiling with sunshine above. At the end of a path, his mum was beckoning, his dad by her side. Her voice came clearly, even though she was several metres away. *"It's okay, Tom,"* she said. *"None of it was your fault. We forgive you, son. We've never stopped loving you."* Tom smiled and started to run towards them. He felt like a 6-year-old again, running down the road after getting off the school bus, his mum standing by the front door, arms wide. He stopped in front of his parents, held out his arms and shut his eyes to hide his tears.

Chapter 25

When he opened his eyes, he was back in the white waiting room. The woman in her white dress and her clipboard stood in front of him. Suddenly she dropped her clipboard, and grabbed him in a tight embrace. He felt warm energy flowing from her. She let go and wiped her tears, not like her usual serene self at all. She picked up her clipboard.

"Hello Tom," she said, a little sheepishly. "What an amazing thing to do. I'm so proud of you. You knew you had to shoot yourself to save someone else's life. And you did it without a second thought."

Tom stayed silent, noticing her blonde hair in its neat bun and her totally creaseless white dress. "Now you know why we couldn't send you back to your adult body," the woman went on. "It had already been taken over by dark forces. We had to give you a new one. We were worried it wouldn't be strong enough. Well, you've proved us wrong!"The woman beamed at him. It was like every part of his body being bathed in sunshine. "So — what now?" asked Tom. "Is that it? Am I dead?"

"Not quite," she said. "It's not completely over yet."

"So I can go back to the people who love me? Sarah, Jason, and Mary — they need me, and I need them. They make me the happiest I've ever been."

She leaned in and kissed his forehead, gently touching his shoulder as she did so. He felt the pain ease. "Rest now, Tom," she said, the light behind her fading. "This will help you recover."

He was falling down a dark tunnel. There was a faint light ahead. He started to run as fast as he could, faster, faster. The woman's voice was behind him: "Run like the wind, Tom. Run like the wind." This was a race he had to win. He sprinted like never before, flat out. His arms pumped through the air, his feet pounded the ground. The light grew closer as he focused everything into one final burst. The light almost blinded him as he coughed and sat bolt upright. He saw his dad, Chris and Tracy grab each other, all of them crying with relief. He'd made it. Back where he belonged. He passed out, safe in the knowledge he was alive.

They finally reached the hospital. A crash team was waiting by the door, ready to take Tom to the emergency theatre. They got him inside as more armed police officers secured the building, along with the PM's bodyguards and members of the elite SAS. Chris Stevens wasn't taking any chances. The Eagle was still out there. He sat with Jason in the waiting room, and watched the story unfold on the television headlines. The prime minister had been shot. The police had recovered a sniper rifle beside the crane, and a trail of blood. The assassin was injured, but not captured. The police hadn't been able to get to him through the crowds.

News reporters and film crews were gathered outside the hospital. A sombre-looking news reporter went live.

"The Prime Minister is still inside, and according to our latest reports, is undergoing emergency surgery. The police believe he was shot by the legendary assassin 'the Eagle', who is still at large. We will continue to update you on any further developments. Our thoughts are with the PM and his family tonight. Back to the studio— no, wait!"

She swung around as a police car screeched to a halt outside the main hospital entrance. Three people exited, two police officers on each side of someone with a blanket over their head. Ignoring the swarming press, they made their way into the hospital.

"We've just witnessed the PM's wife enter the hospital," said the reporter, hoping she was correct. "Okay, back to the studio."

Inside the hospital, Mary took the blanket off as she was shown to the private waiting room. She only had the vaguest information about Tom and her husband, and was half out of her mind. Jason took Mary in his arms and gave her the story as best he could. Chris Stevens was in the room. Mary, moving almost automatically, gave him Tom's letter.

Millions of people across the nation watched the story continue to unfold on TV.

Chapter 26

Two hours later, a happy and relieved surgeon entered the waiting room.

"It's good news," he said. "Tom's stable and in recovery. Luckily, the bullet missed the major brachial artery, or it would have been a very different story. He didn't lose a lot of blood, but it's a miracle he survived the trauma. He's tough as old boots. Once he's out of recovery and in a private room, you can see him. I'll leave you in peace."

"Thank you," Jason said, fervently shaking the surgeon's hand. "Thank you." Mary couldn't find words. Her boy was alive, Sarah was safe, Jason was by her side. Nothing else mattered. Chris Stevens breathed a deep, deep sigh of relief. "Jesus," he said. "Thank God for that. That boy's a bloody hero."

"How's the PM?" asked Jason. "Is he alive?"

"Don't know much," Stevens replied. "He's alive, yes. But anything other than that, the BBC will probably find out before I do. Look, I'll go and ask around. We deserve to know. I'll be back in a bit."

Tom was awake, but kept his eyes closed, thinking back to the moment he had the Eagle in his sights. That split second, when time stood still. The Eagle had looked at him with a sneer, goading him. *You can't shoot me you fool.* Tom had heard the voice clearly, or thought he had. *We'll both die. Go on idiot, pull the fucking trigger. See what happens.*

Tom didn't want to die. He had far too much to live for, a bloody good life. He squeezed the trigger, knowing what was coming. There was no other way. Still, the bullet ripping through his shoulder had been a horrendous experience. Not one he was anxious to repeat.

He opened his eyes. He was lying on a gurney in a sterile recovery room. He almost expected to see the woman in white. Instead, a pleasantly plump little nurse moved into view. "Hello Tom," she said. "How're you feeling?"

"'M'okay, thanks," Tom mumbled, as he shut his eyes and slept once more.

Stevens smiled and raised his hands up high as he came towards Jason and Mary. "You're not going to believe this," he said. "The PM's doing a live press conference outside the hospital in ten fucking minutes. We have to see this. I've read Tom's letter five times, and filled the PM in on all the details. Tom's going to get a knighthood if he's not careful. Happy New Year!" The rumpled detective shook his head, laughing out loud as he switched on the big TV. The PM appeared, a plaster on his head and no other injuries. Tom's aim had been that precise. The bullet had done no more than leave a graze, just as he'd planned.

The PM was in buoyant mood. There was a general election coming up, and this surely stood for more voters. "Well," he began. "Happy New Year, everyone." This got a grumbling laugh as if to say 'Get on with it man."

"As you know already, an attempt has been made to assassinate me," he said. "What you probably don't know is that this attempt was thwarted by a 15-year-old boy, who knocked me out of the way and shot the assassin before he could finish the job.

"The assassin, known as 'the Eagle', is wounded and on the run. Rest assured, we'll leave no stone unturned to hunt him down. In the meantime, this brave boy put his life on the line to save me. He's a courageous and selfless young man, fighting for his life after major surgery to repair a bullet wound. No words can express my gratitude. I owe him my life and my thoughts and prayers are with him and his family. That will be all for now, everyone, I must get back to my family."

The hungry pack of reporters shouted fruitless questions as the PM waved, and went back inside, where he immediately grabbed one of his aides.

"What's this kid's name?" he demanded. "Is he awake yet? Can we get a photo of me by his bed? Come on, man, hop to it! This could win me the election!"

What a dickhead, thought the aide, scurrying off to make arrangements. *Bloody politicians*. He'd spent four years with this arsehole, biting his tongue every day. He had a mortgage, bills to pay. But the PM was without a doubt a selfish, arrogant, bastard. He didn't give a fuck about the boy who saved his life. It was all about votes. Why had the boy bothered to save him? That was a huge question. The aide spoke to the paramedics, the doctors, Chris Stevens and the surgeons while the PM had a fresh plaster put on his head and some powder to take the shine off his nose. Tired and thoroughly pissed off, he made his way back to his boss.

"So, prime minister," he said, slowly, so the stupid man would follow him. "This boy. This boy, who took a bullet and saved your life from the assassin. This boy's heart stopped twice. His body went into shock. He's had emergency surgery to repair the damage. He's stable, but as you can imagine, or maybe you can't, his parents are still sick with worry. This 15-year-old boy, without any doubt, saved your life. Not, sir, with respect, that you care."

The PM, who had been nodding thoughtfully as though listening but was actually planning his next speech for the press, raised his head in surprise. "You, sir," the aide went on, still speaking slowly and levelly, "do not give a flying fuck. All you care about, with respect, is how you can use this incident to gather votes. You, with respect, think it'll win you the election. And so you, prime minister, with respect, can shove your fucking job right up your fucking arse."

The PM watched his now ex-aide turn and walk away. Shrugging his shoulders, he glanced around to see how many people had witnessed his aide's departure. Many of them were definitely smirking. "Someone get me a coffee," he barked. "Then let's sort out this photo by the boy's bed. Bound to make the front page. Then I'm going home, I'm fucking knackered." He looked at his entourage, who were still shuffling. There were one or two definite sniggers. He clapped his hands. "Come on people, what am I paying you for?" he bellowed. "Chop, chop!"

Chapter 27

Tom woke. Instantly, his mind filled with questions. Was his dad okay? Did his mum know he wasn't dead? Was the PM alive? Had they caught the Eagle? When was Sarah coming home? He was in a private room, the window blind closed, but out in the corridor he could see the silhouettes of two armed police officers. His fumbling fingers found the call button and pressed it.

A friendly-looking, vaguely familiar pleasantly-plump nurse appeared. "Good morning, sleepy!" she sang. "How are we feeling today?"

"I'm good thanks — I think," said Tom. He found the water cup by his bed and took a sip or two. "It's — er — it's nice to meet you...?"

The nurse smiled. "We've already met," she said. "But you weren't in much of a condition to remember it, so I won't take it personally. I'm Susan. What can I do for you?"

"I guess, first thing, is can I see my parents, please? They'll be worried sick."

"Just let me get the doc to check you out," she replied. "But I'm sure that won't be a problem, you look fine to me!"

"Wait!" said Tom, as she turned to leave the room. "Is the PM alive? Have they caught the assassin? Is Sarah coming home?"

Susan laughed. "So many questions!" she said. "Yes, the PM's absolutely fine, just a sticking plaster and already up and running press conferences. Unfortunately, they're still looking for the guy that tried to shoot him and managed to shoot you. Hence Tweedledum and Tweedledee out there." She nodded in the direction of the two guards. "I don't know who Sarah is," she finished. "Maybe your mum and dad can help you there. Now, let me go get that doctor." She bustled off, shoes squeaking on the floor.

Half an hour later, after the doc had declared the all-clear, Mary rushed into the room, followed close behind by Jason. Mary fussed over Tom, puffing his pillows up, hugging him gently and crying her eyes out the whole time.

"How're you feeling, son?" said Jason, quietly.

"I'm okay, thanks," said Tom. A little stiff, maybe, but not too bad. Must be some good painkillers, eh? How's Sarah?"

"She's fine, Tom," said Mary. "They're keeping her in the safe house until the Eagle is caught. Can't be too careful, right?

"Chris Stevens is waiting outside," said Jason, looking anxious. "He'd like a word, if you feel up it."

"Sure!" Tom answered, brightly. "I feel fine. Thunderbirds are go!"

Jason beckoned from the doorway, and Chris Stevens entered the room. "Well," he said. "It's good to see you, young man. You had us all worried for a minute there. I've read your letter," he went on, taking a seat on the edge of Tom's bed. Very much not hospital protocol, but he was shattered. He'd been on the go for over 18 hours and he wasn't as young as he used to be.

"Alright," said Tom. "Any questions you need to ask?"

"So many!" laughed Stevens. "But not many relating to your letter — it was really clear. I'm just wondering how clear a look you got at the Eagle?"

"If you can get me some paper and pencils, I'll sketch him for you," said Tom.

Stevens almost ran out of the door, returning ten minutes later with a thick wad of A4 paper and some pencils. "I nearly had to shoot a nurse to get this," he said jokingly, holding up the paper. "Talk about NHS cutbacks!"

"I'll give you a description as I sketch," said Tom. "It'll save time."

Stevens pulled Tom's bed table up and placed the paper on it, handing over a pencil at the same time. It was a little awkward with his left arm in a sling, but Tom set to work.

"He's about six-two," he said, as he sketched. "Short, curly blonde hair, athletic build, rugged face. About 45 or so. Kind of handsome, I suppose, for an old geezer." He winked at Stevens, who grinned back. "Clean-shaven," Tom went on. "Straight white teeth, scar on his face a bit like mine. He was wearing dark-coloured trousers, a black bomber jacket, and black trainers, but he'll have changed by now."

As he spoke, Tom watched the face forming in front of him. The face he used to see in the mirror every day. The man he hated. Himself. His old self. He showed the finished sketch to Stevens.

"We actually met him up close yesterday," he said. "He was in a wheelchair, disguised as an old man. It wasn't until later I realised it was him. I've been kicking myself ever since about that."

"I wouldn't," said Stevens. "No way you could have clocked that. Nobody would. But listen, tell me something," he went on. "Your plan was to shoot him, right? How did you end up shooting the PM?"

"I literally only spotted him at the last minute," said Tom. "And then all I could see was the end of his rifle. I couldn't get a clear shot at the Eagle, so the only way to save the PM was to shoot him myself."

"You were that confident you could shoot to wound at that distance?" said Stevens.

"Oh, yes," said Tom. "I've had loads of practice." He smiled over at Jason. "My dad taught me to shoot. I'm the youngest champion our rifle club's ever had."

"Well, you left the man with nothing but a plaster on his head," said Stevens. "A bloody plaster. You're a living legend, son."

"It was a team effort," said Tom. "I couldn't have done it without my mum and dad. And let's not forget Lisa Miller. She deserves a medal. None of us would have known about the attempt at all if it wasn't for her. She really saved the PM's life."

Taking the sketch, Stevens got up to leave. At the door, he turned and smiled. "If you ever want a job, give me a call," he said.

"Thanks for the offer," said Tom. "But I'm going to be a builder. Like my dad."

Chapter 28

Stevens had no sooner left on his Eagle hunt than another man, to Tom's amazement, popped his head around the door.

"May I enter?" asked the PM. "How's the hero?"

A photographer was lurking behind him. The PM strode past Jason and Mary and stood by the bed, straightening his tie. "You don't mind, do you?" he said, jovially. "Got to commemorate the occasion, you know!"

Jason looked like he was about to punch the man. Tom smiled. "It's okay Dad," he said. "One for the family album, eh? It's not every day we get to meet the Prime Minister."

The PM grinned toothily as the photographer, grumbling about hospital lighting, took several pictures of him heartily shaking Tom's hand. Having got what he wanted, he breezed off, with a cheery "I'll have a copy to sent to you!" Tom wondered how he was going to manage that. He hadn't even bothered to ask his parents' names, never mind how he could get in touch.

The time was 5 am. He looked over at Mary and Jason.

"You guys look worn out," he said. "Please go home and get some sleep. You can pop back later, bring me some real pyjamas."

Mary smiled wearily. "Call me if you need anything," she said, kissing him on the forehead. "We'll see you in a little while."

She picked up her bag and waited by the door. Jason handed Tom his phone.

"Dad, thanks for everything," he said. "You're the best dad in the world. I can't wait to go fishing," he added, yawning. "Bet we catch a great white!"

As Tom drifted back off to sleep, all airports, train stations, ferries and ports in the London area were locked down. There were roadblocks on all major roads. Cars, lorries, vans — everything large enough to conceal a criminal was being searched. No-one was leaving the area, unless they had their own boat or a hot air balloon stashed somewhere. Even then, the coastguard and police helicopter patrols were also on full alert.

Tom's sketch was on the TV news, was already appearing in early editions of the national press. The manhunt was, without question, on

After a few hours of welcome sleep, Tom woke up to find another visitor beside him. He guessed from her uniform that she was the paramedic who had saved his life. "You must be Tracy," he said, holding out his hand. "My dad told me about you. What can I say? Thank you. Just— thank you." Tracy gripped his hand hard and beamed. "Damn, it's good to see you, Tom," she said. "And don't thank me. It's my job. I mean, what kind of paramedic would I be if I let a national hero die? That wouldn't look good on my CV!" Tom laughed, even while his eyes filled with grateful tears. "Dad said you were brilliant," he said, hoarsely. "You never gave up. I can't ever repay you—" Tracy cut him off. "Your dad was a star," she said. "He wouldn't let go of that wound, even when I shocked you. I've never seen anything like it, he barely blinked. If I was the religious type, I'd call it a miracle!" Tom stared at her.

"Thank you for telling me that," he said. "I know my dad never would have. And you know what? I'm just going to think of it as a miracle. I guess someone up there likes me." Tracy smiled, gave his hand one more squeeze and went on her way, a very happy paramedic.

5.30 pm. The surgeon popped in for a chat. Simon Windsor, a friendly sort of guy. He smiled at Tom as he looked over his chart. "How are you feeling, young man?" he said. "The operation went really well, you'll be glad to hear. With a bit of physio once you've healed, your shoulder should work almost perfectly again. Shouldn't think your shooting career will be affected!" he added, chortling. "Plus you'll have a brilliant scar to show your friends."

Thanking the man for his help, Tom asked the question uppermost in his mind. "When can I go home, doctor?" he said. "I really think I'll recover much faster there — I know my mum will take good care of me. And I want to see my girlfriend — I'm missing her like crazy."

"Well, ideally I'd keep you in for another few days," said Windsor, hastily adding as Tom's face fell, "But as you seem to be doing so well and the wound looks so good — honestly, it almost looks like it's healing already — let's say one more night for observation, and we'll review the situation tomorrow. If all's well, and we set up regular check-ups, you might well be able to go home."

"Brilliant," said Tom. "Thanks so much. I'm sure I'll feel even better after a good night's sleep. Oh!" he added, as the man turned to go. "Can I have the bullet? I'd like to keep it, as a memento."

"Sorry Tom," said the surgeon. "Police have it. Forensics, you know? They have to check it against the Eagle's rifle. You might be able to get it once all this is over."

Tom nodded, disguising a small, nagging concern. He knew the police would have the Kalashnikov, and now they had the bullet. It was only a matter of time until they put two and two together. This wasn't good news. At 6.30 pm Chris Stevens returned, looking happy. The forensic team had found the bullet that had grazed the PM embedded in the deck of the barge.

"Hi Tom!" he almost chirped. "Your mum and dad are on their way — I know because two of my guys are with them at all times. I wasn't going to ask you how you're feeling, cause I know what it's like to be shot, but you look surprisingly well!"

"I feel good," said Tom. "What can I say? I'm a fast healer. Any news on the Eagle?"

He wanted his Sarah back — that's what this had all been about, after all. Stevens shook his head.

"What about fingerprints on his rifle?" Tom went on. "Or DNA from the blood?"

"We've got both, Tom. Weird that he wasn't wearing gloves, I'd have expected him to. And we have DNA, but he's not on record anywhere. Still, we've enough evidence to charge him and bang him up for a long stretch once he's caught." He looked at Tom for a moment, head on one side. "What do you think?" he said, thoughtfully. "Where do you think he might be? Where would he hide?"

"Ha — that's the million-dollar question!" said Tom. "But my gut instinct is that he's not too far away, probably closer than we think. Look, I have an idea. Let's set a trap."

"I'm all ears," said Stevens. "But remember, your safety comes first. Enough hero stuff, okay?"

"It's a pretty simple plan, sir," said Tom. "It only needs two things from you, and a little bit of luck."

Tom outlined his idea. It was based on what they both already knew — that if the Eagle was alive, he'd be coming after Tom. "No way," said Stevens. "Absolutely no way. It's too risky. Your mother would murder me. I don't even want to think about what your Dad would do to me."

"Trust me, sir," said Tom. "You have to trust me. You have to have faith."

Chapter 29

Two hours later, with Jason and Mary by his side, Tom watched the hastily-called press conference outside the hospital. Stevens had been right, the look on her face when they told her the plan promised bloody murder. But they'd convinced her.

"Listen mum," Tom had said, quietly but firmly. "We can't have this hanging over us. We'll spend the rest of our lives looking over our shoulders. I can't let that happen. This way, we control the situation. It's actually safer than just walking out of here, even with an armed guard. Do you want those guys surrounding the house for the rest of our lives? No. We have to finish it. Then we can live our lives in peace."

Mary and Jason had reluctantly agreed. Now Stevens stood in front of the hungry reporters and reeled off a short speech.

"Ladies and gentlemen," he said. "The Eagle, the world's most wanted criminal, has been captured and is in police custody right now. And it's all thanks to one young man — Thomas Drake. You know he foiled a conspiracy to assassinate the PM. That he sustained a bullet wound and needed major emergency surgery. You know he appeared to pull through. Sadly, I have to tell you tonight that his condition took a sudden turn for the worse, and he's lapsed into a coma as the result of complications in the recovery process. Right now, he's fighting for his life and we're not sure if he'll make it through the night. I'm sure you'll join me in wishing him, and his family, all the luck in the world. We'll keep you informed of events. That's all I can tell you right now. Sorry, no questions."

Stevens bowed his head and ran back into the hospital as reporters screamed questions after him. He'd briefed his commanding officer before the announcement. Orders had been given. Slowly and conspicuously, the police presence withdrew from the hospital and drove away. Most of the camera crews and reporters remained, waiting for the next update.

Back in his room, Tom was tucking into Mary's home cooking. "Thanks, Mum," he said, as he polished off the last bite of lasagne. "I needed that. I'm so looking forward to coming home — hospital food just can't stand up to your cooking." Seeing her worried look, he went on, "Try not to worry, Mum. I know it's hard, but honestly, we've got this covered. It's the best way." He yawned. "Try to get some sleep tonight. I'm just going to text Sarah, then have a rest myself."

"I texted Sarah earlier," said Mary. "The poor girl's going out of her mind. The sooner she's back home with us, the better."

"Couldn't agree more," said Tom. "Won't be long now. G'night, you guys. I love you both."

"Goodnight, son," said Jason, handing Tom his rucksack. "Your clothes are in here. Mum ironed your socks again. I tried to stop her, but you know mum."

Tom grinned as his parents hugged him goodbye and headed home.

Stevens came back to the room, carrying the two items Tom had requested. "Good luck, son," he said. "I bloody hope this works. Got the button ready? Good. Press that bastard the second you need me."

Finally, Tom had the room to himself. His phone lit up — Sarah. He smiled as he opened the message.

What's going on? Your mum said you were fine, but I've just watched the news - are you OK? Please answer RIGHT NOW, I'm going out of my mind!

Sarah, it's OK, I'm fine. All part of a plan. How are *you*?

I'd be better if I was with you. What's going on?

I promise you I'm okay. I can't tell you much more right now, but please, don't worry. Everything is under control.

Oh God, this is a nightmare. I should be with you.

Stay strong, Sarah. We'll be together soon. I'm sending you a hug. I have to go right now, but I'll text again really soon, OK?

OK, Tom. Don't you dare die on me or anything. I love you.

Thanks, Sarah, I love you too.

Sarah dried her tears and, once again, turned to her diary for comfort.

Dear brave and beautiful Tom. I'm so happy you're alive, I can't even put it into words. I can't lose you. I've already lost far too many people that I love. I hope Jason and Mary are okay. I promise that from now on I'll look after all three of you for as long as I live. And Lisa. I know you'll help me take care of Lisa. Oh God, I need to be with you, I need to be by your side. You're my hero. I'll never stop loving you. You came into my life when I needed you the most, you saved me. You're the bravest man I've ever met. I don't feel sad or lonely when I'm with you. It always feels like the sun is shining on my face. It's magical. I'm going to make you proud of me, Tom. I can see it. I can see our future, and it gives me hope. We'll have a happy home. We'll have love and laughter all our lives. Those doctors and nurses had better be looking after you, or they'll have me to deal with. All my love, always and always.

Tom turned his phone off and put it under his pillow, next to the pocket bible Jason had, for some reason, put into his knapsack. Something was going to happen soon, he could feel it. He closed his eyes as the door slowly opened.

A tall man entered the room. He stood over the motionless boy, glaring. In one lightning-fast move, he grabbed Tom's pillow from under his head and pressed it down hard over his face. "You should have kept your nose out of my business," he whispered. "Now you pay the price."

Tom counted to ten, then made his first move. His right hand shot up, pepper spray aimed as best he could. A direct hit. The man let go of the pillow and stumbled backwards, hands covering his face. Tom sat up, a police-issue Taser gun in his hand. He aimed and squeezed the trigger. The Eagle went down. Tom felt the current hit him as the man jerked on the floor. He couldn't see, his eyes blinded by the pepper spray. Frantically, he pressed the call button, which they'd taped to his strapped-up left hand. He just hoped they'd respond on time.

Chapter 30

Stevens stormed into the room, gun in hand, to see a man lying on the floor, shaking violently, his eyes red and streaming. Knocking the Taser from Tom's hand, he leapt onto the man before he had a chance to recover. Not that he was likely to, Tom had kept his finger clamped onto the fire button and the man was doubtless in shock. Still, better not to take chances. Flipping his captive with strength he didn't know he had, Stevens pulled out his cuffs and quickly secured him, then screamed into his radio.

"Greenlight! Go! Go! Go!"

Four armed officers rushed into the room and grabbed a limb each. Stevens let them take over shackling the prisoner, while he checked on Tom. The boy was lying on his bed, panting and shaking, eyes streaming and a horrifying red. "What happened?" demanded Stevens. "Are you alright?"

"I'm okay," gasped Tom. "Just a bit of backfire from the pepper spray. And I think your Taser might be faulty, I feel like it got me, too. Did it work? Did we get him?"

"Oh, it bloody worked alright," said Stevens, triumphantly. "All trussed up like a Christmas turkey, ready for transport. Lovely stuff. See?"

"Can't see a thing, sir," said Tom. "But I'll take your word for it."

Stevens stood back from the bed and watched his officers drag the stunned and shackled man away. "Jesus," he said, quietly. "We only caught the world's most wanted criminal. Now that's a good start to the year."

Sending one of his men for a nurse to bathe Tom's eyes, Stevens sat back in the visitor chair. Time for a quick breather before heading down to the station. Not as young as I was, he thought, ruefully. Still. Got the bugger. He grinned to himself.

"Sir?" Tom's voice brought him back to himself. "When can Sarah come home? And what's going to happen to her mum now? She's a good woman, you know. It's down to her we've pulled this off."

"That's down to the crown prosecution service," Stevens replied. "If I had my way, she'd be a free woman. She gave us so much info about George Miller's activities – not just this assassination plot. There are a lot of people who'll be feeling very nervous about what we know, right now. So that'll help her case a bit. Can't say more than that.

"About Sarah — I'll make the call right now, while you call your mum to tell her you're safe. Then try to get some rest, alright?"

Tom was already dialling as Stevens left the room. Stevens made the promised call to Sarah's minders, and set off down the corridor. "What a kid," he thought. "Bloody bright. Fearless, too. Wonder if him and Rich would get on..." Rich was Stevens' own son. He didn't see him much, since the divorce. Time for that to change, maybe? He pulled out his phone.

"Happy New Year, son," he said, when Rich picked up. "How are you? How's your mum? Sorry, should have phoned earlier, been a bit busy these last 12 hours or so."

"I know!" said his son's voice. "We saw you on the news. You were brilliant, Dad. Like Sherlock Holmes or something. Even mum was impressed. How's that boy? Tom, is it?

"He's great, son, doing just fine. I'll fill you in on the whole story soon, yeah? I'd like to spend more time with you. It's taken me a long while to realise this, son, but I can see now that I've been putting my job first and you second, and I'm really sorry for that. I hope you and your mum will forgive me one day."

"Nothing to forgive, Dad. Your work's important. But yeah, let's spend more time together. I'd like that. I— wait, hold on a mo..."

Stevens heard muffled voices in the background, then Rich came back on the line. "Mum said please come over and have supper with us, anytime you like. We'd both love to see you. We'll need to have a chat about getting you on Celebrity Big Brother, or into the jungle on I'm a Celebrity, Get Me Out Of Here!"

They both laughed. "You're on," said Stevens. "I'll call as soon as all this is wrapped up and we'll arrange it. Great to speak to you son. I love you."

He had one more thing to do before heading to the station. He phoned Jason, then called his boss. Both agreed. Job done.

Tom opened his eyes to the now-familiar white waiting room. The Woman in White, as he was now thinking of her, stood by his side as he lay on a bed that felt like lying on a cloud. "Well," she said. "How's the hero?"

"I'm bloody knackered, to be honest," said Tom. "Tell me this is almost over!"

"Just one last thing to do," she said. "We need to disconnect you from your other half, for want of a better phrase, in case anything happens to him. I'm pretty sure it will. Wish we could have done it sooner, but we had to wait until you caught him and finished the job."

"You mean that's it?" said Tom. "I'm done?"

She nodded. "You're done," she said. "Now, lie back and close your eyes, please."

A warmth flooded through Tom's body and mind, a feeling of being washed absolutely, spiritually and physically clean. He'd never felt so at peace in his life. He was aware of floating gently downwards, and knew his connection with this room and this woman was coming to an end.

"Will I ever see you again?" he murmured.

"Yes Tom," came her whispered reply. "I'm quite sure you will. Now, goodbye, Thomas Drake. Take good care."

Chapter 31

2nd January.

Tom sat in the hospital shower, a large basin of hot water in front of him, from which he was having a very satisfying wash. The nurse had wanted to come in with him, but he'd rebelled. He'd allowed them to leave the door open, but other than that he was drawing the line. He accepted their help getting dressed, though. Socks and laces are tricky when you only have one working hand.

A friendly nurse came by to check his blood pressure and update his charts, and said the surgeon would be around in an hour or so. He lay on the bed and waited, flicking through news reports on his phone. Eventually, Dr Windsor arrived to check his wound and whatever else it was he checked off on that baffling chart. He shook his head, and for a moment Tom's heart sank.

"I just don't get it," said the surgeon. "It's not even been 48 hours, but this wound looks like it's about a week old. It's healing beautifully. I just wish I knew why!" He looked at Tom, who was sitting up hopefully, phone in hand. "Go ahead and phone your folks, Tom," he said. "I'll tell you, if we could bottle whatever it is you've got, some of us would be right out of a job in no time!" He shook Tom's hand, accepted his thanks, and walked off to see to his next patient.

A nurse came and redressed his wound, helped him get his shirt back on and pack his bag. His left shoulder was stiff and his arm movement was restricted, but it didn't hurt much. By 8.30am, he was ready to go. Suddenly, Chris Stevens appeared at the door.

"Morning Tom," he said, rubbing his hands together. "All set? I've got a car waiting."

"Morning sir," said a surprised Tom. "I'm expecting my dad any second now..."

"Change of plan," said Stevens, beaming at him. "I have a surprise for you. Come on, let's get the hell out of here. Oh, and Tom?"

"Yes, sir?"

"Stop calling me 'sir', will you? The name's Chris."

He picked up Tom's bag. Side by side, they walked out of the hospital and got into waiting police car, a huge cordon of dark-blue uniforms holding back the press, then set off, lights flashing and sirens on. Tom quickly realised they weren't heading towards Richmond. They were on the M25, doing an alarming rate.

"Er... where are we going, Chris?" said Tom.

"Heathrow Airport. I think you can guess why."

Tom nodded and smiled. This was a good start to the day.

The car roared into the airport, and parked in front of the terminal building. Chris was by Tom's side as they walked through the terminal, flanked by two armed officers from the airport. It was all for show, just a bit of theatre. People moved out of the way and applauded as they went past. News travels fast.

They waited by the arrivals gate, Tom bouncing on his toes with excitement. At last. Sarah. She spotted Tom immediately, and ran right into his one outstretched arm. Holding his face with both hands, she kissed him fiercely, right on the lips. The crowd burst into applause. Women were openly crying. Even Chris had a lump in his throat.

Jason and Mary were waiting to welcome them home. Chris carried the luggage inside, then said his farewells — time he caught up with his own family. His job was done for now. Four very happy people gathered around the fire in the lounge to enjoy their reunion. Mary handed Sarah a little gift bag, which she opened eagerly. It was a paint colour chart. Sarah looked at Mary quizzically. "Time we sorted that bedroom out for you," Mary said — and signed. She'd been practicing to get it right. "This is to help you choose your colours."

Sarah leapt to her feet and wrapped Mary in a massive hug, then turned to Jason, who was already holding out an interior design magazine.

"Thought this might be handy, too," he said, dropping the magazine and swinging the delighted girl around, much to everyone's amusement.

Tom got up, stiffly, heading for the downstairs loo. As he came out again, he passed the kitchen. The snowman, only slightly melted, was still smiling in the window. And a family of four robins was busily feeding from his hat.

Chapter 32

The time was 9 pm. Tom and Sarah said goodnight and, side by side, hand in hand, climbed the stairs for bed. Mary was right behind them. She helped Sarah to brush out her long blonde hair, and tucked her in with a kiss. "Mary, I'm so grateful," said the girl. "I'll never be able to thank you enough."

"No need to thank us," said Mary. "This is your home now, you are part of our family. And we're so happy to have you. Goodnight, princess. Sweet dreams."

Mary quietly stepped along to Tom's room, where she helped him into his pyjama top, and tucked him in tightly. "It's good to be home, Mum," he said.

"It's good to have you home, Tom," said Mary. "I was scared to death it might not happen for a minute there. Let's keep things calm for a little while, shall we?"

Tom nodded fervently. "Sounds good to me," he said. "Goodnight, Mum."

As Mary made her way downstairs, Sarah opened her diary. She smiled as she wrote.

Dear Mary. You remind me so much of my mum. She would be happy to know I'm safe and loved. When you brushed my hair, it was like going back in time, like being six years old again, with my own mum brushing my hair. I'm going to be the best daughter to you. When you're old, I'm going to look after you. I'll brush your hair. Buy you clothes, tidy your room, cook delicious food for you. But we'll have loads of happy years together before then. I want you to help me pick out my wedding dress when Tom and I finally get married. I want Jason to walk me down the aisle. I want both of you to enjoy your grandchildren, and to live near us forever. It's fantastic to finally be home.

Sarah closed her diary, and lay back in bed. All those years of abuse, she thought. All those different people, making me miserable. Until I met Tom.

Sarah sent a text. She needed to be beside Tom tonight, to make sure he was really okay, really there by her side.

Can I join you?

Of course. Just mind the squeaky door and creaky floorboards.

I'll tiptoe.

Downstairs, Mary smiled at Jason. *"Did you hear that?"* she said.

"Hear what?"

"That creaky floorboard. It's Sarah, sneaking through to see Tom. You know they sometimes sleep together? I'm not sure if it's a good thing or a bad thing. It's adorable, but it's a little bit worrying too. They're both still very young."

"Ah, let them be," said Jason. "I trust Tom. After everything we've just been through, I'm pretty sure he'd talk to us if things with Sarah were getting... you know. Physical. Besides, it's been an ordeal. I'd get in beside them both myself if it wasn't just flat out weird."

Mary smiled at him, her eyes sparkling. "Oh well," she said, moving closer. "You'll just have to make do with me."

Chapter 33

3rd January. 7.30 am.

Tom was first up. He took off his sling off, quietly went downstairs and set coffee on to brew, gathering his thoughts. This was going to be a big day. Chris Stevens had called Jason yesterday afternoon. The Eagle was in court today. Tom wanted to see him up close. So they were all going to London for the day. When Mary and Jason came down, he shared his plans with them. "If that's okay with you, of course," he finished. "I just really want to surprise Sarah after we've been to court."

"You're still sure you want to go to court?" said Mary.

"Yes. I feel like I need to, somehow," said Tom. "I don't think it'll take long. I just want to see him up close to. It'll be quite safe," he added. "He can't harm me in the courtroom. Besides, Chris Stevens will be there."

"Alright," said Mary. "Let's get into action mode. No, wait, not action mode. No more of that. Let's just get going, alright?"

They reached the station with 10 minutes to spare, Tom's arm back in its sling and his school satchel over his good shoulder. He sat next to Sarah and texted as they waited for the train.

We have a surprise for you later.

I love surprises. What is it?

If I *told* you, it wouldn't be a *surprise*.

Just teasing.

I'll text you when we're leaving court.

Cool. Try NOT to get shot today, okay?

I'll do my best. Here comes the train. Want the window seat?

Tom, look at your mum and dad. It's so cute. They're holding hands.

They looked at each other and giggled, a pair of naughty children. Just as they should be, thought Mary, smiling serenely at them.

They enjoyed the fast train ride to London, Sarah especially. She'd never been to the capital. Chris Stevens met them at Waterloo, and he and Tom headed off to the Old Bailey. Jason, Mary and Sarah headed for the bus stop. They were going to take the City Tour, show Sarah all the sights.

Chris and Tom entered the court through a side door, away from the press. They sat in a private room, waiting for the case to be called. "This won't take long," said Chris. "He doesn't have much choice in the matter. The case against him is watertight. He's going down for a long stretch, whatever he says."

"Have you spoken to him?" asked Tom. "What's he like?"

"I've interviewed him, yes. He is not a nice person. Something weird about him. Empty. Obviously a total sociopath. At least that means a jury isn't likely to sympathise with him, if he's mental enough to go to trial."

A policeman appeared at the door. "All set boss," he said. "Court number one."

The courtroom was packed. Thankfully, Chris's colleagues had held a couple of seats for him and Tom. It put him right in line with the dock. He'd have a clear view of the Eagle for the first time. The suspect was brought into court, his black soulless eyes locking almost instantly on Tom. Tom didn't flinch. Time to face his fears head-on, and this was a big one — facing the man he used to be.

"All rise," said the clerk.

Chapter 34

Silence fell as the judge entered the courtroom. The atmosphere was electric. Reporters were poised, notebooks at the ready. The judge sat, and the rest of the court followed suit. Tom sat dead still, hardly breathing.

The hearing was short, as expected. The Eagle pleaded guilty. There would be no trial. Cheers from the crowd. As two burly guards stepped forward to take the prisoner back to the cells, he turned to face Tom. "You're dead," he mouthed. "I'm going to kill you." Tom held his stare. He saw the raging flames of hell burn in the depths of those eyes, the eternal torment of the twisted mind. He shrugged, gave the man a wink and a jaunty wave goodbye.

"Well," he said, on the way out. "That's that. I'm glad I saw him. Now I know what pure evil looks like." Stevens nodded. "You're not wrong," he said. "If looks could kill, we'd be in big trouble." They made their way back to the police car in silence.

"Tom," said Stevens, after they were safely belted in and edging out into the gridlocked traffic. "I'm wondering if you can help me with something else. It's doing my head in." Tom closed his eyes for a second. Here we go, he thought. "We've got the forensics in," said Stevens. "Some really, really weird results."

Tom stayed silent.

"We had to fire both weapons for testing and evidence purposes, right? Now, here's the thing. The bullet fired from the Kalashnikov matches the bullet from the barge deck. So far, so good. But it also matches the one that came out of your shoulder, the one we thought had come from his rifle. In fact, it turns out, his weapon hadn't even been fired that night. So...?"

"Hmm," said Tom, pretending to think it through. "What about the bullet that hit him?" he asked. "Did you find that?"

"No, that one wasn't recovered. It seems to have gone right through."

"I see. So – this might sound mental, but bear with me — is it at all possible that the bullet went through him, hit the crane and ricocheted back into me?"

Stevens gaped at him. "Who are you, JFK?" he said. "No, that's just — It's not — Nah, it can't be... Can it?"

"I don't know," said Tom. "I don't know too much about ballistics outside a firing range. And I don't really remember much about that night. It's all a bit hazy. Does it matter? If he's pleading guilty anyway?"

"Not really, I suppose," said Stevens. "It's just a puzzle, that's all. Going to be niggling at me the rest of my life, that one. Still, we bloody nailed him. I guess that's what's important..." He trailed off, then seemed to give himself a little shake. "Alright my son, as we say in the Force," he said, jovial once again. "Let's get you reunited with your family. London Eye, Dave!" he called to the driver. "Alligator speed!"

"What's alligator speed?" said Dave.

Tom and Stevens answered together. "Make it snappy!"

Siren on and lights flashing, they dropped Tom off at the London Eye. Stevens was still laughing as he waved and drove away. Tom joined his family at the front of the long queue.

"How did it go?" said Mary, examining him anxiously.

"All good, mum," said Tom. "The Eagle's wings are well and truly clipped."

"Thank God!" said Jason and Mary at the same moment. Tom put his arm round Sarah and smiled. He kept it there as they got into their pod and prepared to move. "Don't look down on the way up," he said. "You'll get dizzy. Stay focused on the horizon. The view's amazing from the top."

And it was.

Chapter 35

"Any plans for tomorrow, Tom?" said Mary, that night. "Because Sarah and I are going into town. Do you need anything?"

"I'll come with you if we can go in early," said Tom. "I only need to pop into the discount shop. Then Dad and I are going fishing."

"I've already looked out the rods," said Jason. "But it's freezing son, and it's out of season. We probably won't catch anything, you know."

"Sounds perfect, doesn't it?" said Tom, laughing.

"You know what son," said Jason, giving him a gentle squeeze, "It really does."

Sarah was upstairs, rummaging through her old school bag. It had been left at the Drakes' while she was away. Suddenly, her hand closed around a large roll of what felt like paper, and emerged holding a huge wedge of cash. "Oh my God!" She ran into Tom's room and dropped it on his desk.

"Look, Tom!" she said. "I forgot about the money Lisa put in my bag! I never thought it would be this much! Where did she get it from? I've never seen so much money in my life! I'm going to give it to Mary and Jason — they've already spent so much on me, and my school fees need paying, I saw an overdue invoice."

"Alright, Sarah," said Tom, putting his good arm around her to calm her. "Let's see what Mum and Dad have to say. I don't think they'll take it, but let's not argue about it. Get Mum to open a savings account somewhere, one with a nice rate of interest. We'll call it rainy day money. Everyone should have some of that."

Sarah looked at him. "You know what's weird?" she said. "There were two rolls of cash. This one —" she pointed to the roll on the desk — "And this one." She held out her hand. In it was the £250 Lisa had stashed in her bag. Tom shrugged with one shoulder. "Maybe she found an extra little stash somewhere after she'd put the first lot in?" he said. "Maybe

George left it lying about and she just decided to throw it in too? Who knows? Either way, it gives you the beginnings of a nice little nest egg."

"Nest egg!" laughed Sarah. "What are you, 40 years old?"

Jason was sitting in the garage, sorting through a box of baits and hooks and other fishing paraphernalia when Tom came in and sat on a fishing box. "Hi Dad," said the boy, his handsome face serious. "Can we talk, please?"

"Of course," said Jason. "What's on your mind?"

"I need some advice. Say someone was mean to mum. Pushed her about and called her names. What would you do?"

"Is this about school? Is that what the kids do to Sarah?"

"Yeah. I feel bad about it. I don't mind them calling me names, but it makes me really angry when they do it to her. How can I make them stop?"

"Look, Tom," said Jason, fists unconsciously clenching. "You know I believe violence is the last resort. But sometimes people just need a short sharp shock. Whatever you do, I'll back you. Would it help if I had a chat with the headmaster before term starts properly?"

"Mum asked the same thing," said Tom. "But I think it would just make matters worse and the teachers can't be there all the time. I'll just have to deal with it myself. But it's good to know you'll be there for me, whatever happens."

Jason nodded. "Whatever happens," he agreed. "Right, son. Let's get back inside. We're ready for tomorrow. Right now, it's almost time for supper — bangers and mash await!"

After supper, while Tom and Jason cleaned up, Sarah gave the £5k in cash to Mary. When she got over the shock, and convinced Sarah she wouldn't take the money, they agreed that they'd use it to open a savings account, and could use some of the money from it to buy Lisa anything she needed. Jason had also spoken to his solicitor friend, so her case was in good hands.

At 9 pm, it was time for bed and, as usual, Mary tucked them both in. At 9.30 pm, Sarah sent a text to Tom.

Thanks for today. It was a special surprise.

Glad you enjoyed yourself.

I can't believe how lucky I am.

That's how I feel every day. Lucky.

It's so great not to feel lonely any more.

Mary seems even happier now you're here. I could hear her singing in the kitchen while you both made supper

I made the mash myself.

Ah, that explains why it was so good. The best part of the meal.

A Night, Tom. Love you. x

A Night Sarah. Love you too. x

Two very happy people shut their eyes and slept.

Chapter 36

4th January. 6 am.

Tom woke, but decided to have a lie-in. He wanted to think about how he was going to deal with those bullies at school. He knew what he wanted to do — punch the ringleader right on the nose — but he felt like there must be a better solution.

His thoughts drifted to the day's plans. If he was in town by 9.30, and back by 10.30, he and Jason would have plenty of fishing time together before it got dark. Right on cue, he heard his father walk downstairs. No matter how hard Jason tried to be quiet, his size twelves going down the stairs always sounded like the Jolly Green Giant.

Tom got up and followed the echoes into the kitchen. "Got it all planned out, Dad," he said.

"What?" said a still-sleepy Jason. "Needa coffee. Whatsa plan?"

Tom laughed at his dishevelled parent. "There's plenty of time, Dad," he said. "Get your coffee sorted. I'm thinking if we take both cars to town, you and mum can go for a cuppa while Sarah and me nip to the discount shop. We don't need much, just pens, pencils, notepads, that kind of thing. Then we can leave Mum and Sarah in town, and head out fishing. Sound good?"

Jason nodded, helpless in the face of Tom's precision planning. "Fine by me, Tom," he mumbled, turning back to the coffee machine.

They reached the town centre at 9.15 am and easily found a parking spot. Jason and Mary went to the café, while Tom and Sarah went to the discount store. As they walked out of the shop, hand in hand, Tom stopped dead. A hulking 17-year-old boy stood in their way, two mates behind him. Bullying season had started early. He kept quiet, standing his ground.

"Hi Scarface," said the boy. "HI, DEAF EARS! Aw, look lads. The nerds are holding hands. It's so sweet. Cat got your tongue, Tommy?" he said, when he failed to get a reaction. "You make the perfect couple, don't you? Deaf and dumb."

The bully looked at his mates, who laughed dutifully, then turned his attention back to Tom. "The big brave hero," he said, in a mocking voice. "The boy who saved the PM... Not so brave now, are you?"

Tom glanced at his watch. Fuck it. He'd reached his limit.

"Look, asshole," he said. "You decide what happens next. Get out of our way, or I'm going to deck you. Up to you."

The boy pushed Tom on his bad shoulder, and laughed. Tom took a breath and a shape flew past him, blurred by speed. Sarah struck like a snake, her dainty little foot connecting right where it wanted to go. As the boy went down, Tom let rip with a mighty right-hand uppercut. The bully hit the pavement, blood dribbling from his mouth, hands clamped around his groin. A lesson learned the hard way.

The other boys stepped back. Tom bent down so he was close to the bully's ear. "You play with fire, you get burned," he said, in his most menacing grown-up Glaswegian voice. "I hope you've learned your lesson, boy. Stay out of our way. I see you bullying anyone, ever again, I'll break your fucking nose and ram the rest of your teeth down your fucking throat." He stepped back. "Up to you," he said, and turned to walk away. He and Sarah high-fived as the two goons tried to help their fallen leader to his feet.

An hour later, Tom sat on a fishing stool next to his dad. They'd chipped a hole in the frozen lake for appearance's sake, but neither of them was bothered. There wasn't even any bait on Jason's hook. It was so peaceful, just the sound of winter birds piping and the water under the broken ice.

Jason was bursting with pride. They sat in silence, no need for words, as the sky went from grey to gold, from gold to red. As darkness fell, they reluctantly packed up and drove towards town. "Fishmongers, Dad?"

"That's the plan son. Can't go home empty-handed. Mum and Sarah would wonder what we've been doing all afternoon."

Tom knew how happy Jason was. He also thought he might be borderline insane. No one in their right mind goes fishing in -2 degrees. His feet were bloody freezing. He'd have to borrow Mary's bed socks next time.

They unloaded the gear in the garage, then went inside the warm house.

Chapter 37

An excited Sarah came dancing out to meet them, twirling in a new dress. "What do you think?" she said, blushing furiously. "Wow!" said Tom, shrugging off his three overcoats and peeling off two pairs of gloves. "You look stunning – the prettiest girl on this planet!"

Sarah blushed and showed him her painted nails, red with little sparkles at the tips. She moved her fingers, they glittered in the light. Jason left Tom lost in admiration and took the huge salmon he'd just bought into the kitchen.

"Hello Mary!" he boomed. "Wow!" he added, taking a lesson from his son. "I love your hair — you look sensational! Here we go, my love — one salmon, proudly provided by the fishermen!"

"Well done," said Mary, smiling slyly at him. "And that's a trout pond too. Who'd have thought it?"

"Who, indeed?" said Jason, heading off to get cleaned up.

Mary and Sarah had been busy after getting home from town. Mary had bought a large scrapbook, and several sticks of glue. Together, she and Sarah had sifted through all the accumulated newspapers from the past few days, and cut out every story about Tom. One, in particular, caught Mary's attention. It was from the paramedic, Tracy. She told her story about trying to keep Tom alive in the ambulance after he'd been shot. About how Jason had held the wadding tight and wouldn't let go, even when Tracy sent electricity racing through Tom's body. Her incredible man had saved their son's life. She didn't think she'd ever felt so proud.

They all enjoyed the salmon, cooked by Jason, the hunter-gatherer. Tom and Sarah helped clean up afterwards. It took longer than usual — Jason was a good cook, but he wasn't a tidy one. Afterwards, Mary grabbed the chance for a quick chat with Tom, while Jason and Sarah argued good-naturedly over the evening's movie choice.

"All set for school?" she said. "Homework done?"

"Yep, everything's good," replied Tom. "Homework all ready to hand in on Monday. Sarah's essay is way better than mine. I'll have to pull my socks up."

"Are you worried?" said Mary. "About going back to school, I mean?"

"Actually, no, Mum," said Tom, with a confident smile. "That's all under control." He looked over at Sarah, and smiled. "Tell you what, though," he said. "I'll be bloomin' careful not to make her angry!"

Dear Mum, Dad, and Clare, Sarah wrote that night. *I've had the most amazing day. Mary took me to town, bought me a new school uniform. And wow! A first for me —I had my hair and nails done. Tom was fishing with his dad, so it was just us girls. It just felt amazing. We chatted, giggled — it was so lovely. I've been lonely for far too long. Mary, Jason, and Tom have saved me. They've set me free. I'm not going to feel guilty any more. I can't spend the rest of my life feeling like that. I have to grasp this amazing new life and hang onto it for as long as I can. Every minute of every day, I'll be the best I can be. I have a chance to find the happiness you'd all want me to have. Tom and I are a team — we even sorted out the school bullies today. I love him. I love Jason and Mary. And I love you.*

Chapter 38

5th January.

Tom and Sarah had done their own washing and drying. Since Tom only had one good arm, Sarah did the ironing. Tom hid his socks. Fully kitted out, they were ready for tomorrow. Tom, packing his school bag, checked to make sure he'd put his bible inside. He always took it to school. He wasn't sure why.

"I'm going to be redundant," said Mary to Jason. "They don't need me anymore."

"I think it's brilliant," said Jason. "Those kids bloody love you. And they'll always need you, that I know. So enjoy it. Spend more time doing the things you like. Get to the leisure centre if you want to. Make some new friends. Do some things for yourself — you already do more than enough for us."

"I might take up tennis again," said Mary, musingly. "Want to join me? We'll need new kit. But I think we'll be able to afford it, don't you?"

Jason kissed his beautiful wife. While the story about the assassination attempt had flashed through the media, his estate agent had added a few extra 'for sale' signs around the building that was at the centre of the news. The estate agent was a wise man.

The media story had basically been a massive amount of free advertising. Monday morning was going to see a stampede of viewings, and the prospect for more was good. The agent was confident all the apartments would be sold within the month. A good start to the year.

The only cloud still on their horizon was worry about Lisa. They'd been back to Oak Tree Farm so Sarah could collect the last of her belongings. Not that there was much. The place looked even shabbier and more desolate after what had happened. Sarah had been visibly upset. She'd hated the place, hated George. But she'd loved Lisa, and the thought of her fate was a hard one.

That evening, sitting by the fire, Sarah squeezed Tom's hand. "I'm going to visit Lisa soon," she signed. "Will you please come with me?"

"Of course!" he replied. "As long as I'm allowed."

"I think it'll be okay. I asked her to put you on her visitors' list."

"No problem, then," he said. "Anything to help you, Sarah."

"One other thing," she added, hands and fingers flying while a huge blush overspread her pretty face. "It's about tomorrow."

Tom looked at her expectantly.

"Can I— tell people you're my boyfriend?"

Tom laughed. "Of course!" he said. "I'm proud that I'm your boyfriend. I'm the luckiest person in the whole school!"

"No," said Sarah.

"What do you mean, Sarah? Why do you say that?"

"Because I'm the luckiest person in school."

Tom smiled. "We'll be the luckiest people together," he said.

Chapter 39

6th January. Back to school.

7.30 am. Tom and Sarah were ready for school. Jason had already left for work, ready to make those sales and reclaim his passion for building. He was back, big time. It was time to finish up on this site, and start looking for the right spot for his first dream village.

Everyone else was sitting at the kitchen table eating porridge. Tom was trying to keep the mood light.

"Who's been eating *my* porridge?" he roared.

He burst out laughing at their blank faces. *"My porridge?"* he said. "The three bears? No?"

Light dawned. "Dunno who'd want to eat your porridge, you daft bear," said Sarah. "You put *salt* on it. Yuck!"

"Better than *syrup*," said Tom, pulling a disgusted face. "Bleargh!"

The banter continued until their coats went on at 8.30 and they got ready to leave the house. "Here we go then!" said Tom. "Right, young lady, no *kicking* off today!" he teased.

"I'll give it my best *shot*," she fired back.

Mary drove them to school. Normally they'd walk, but today Mary had plans and no time to waste. She was going to the Leisure Centre for the first time in ages. A cardio workout, maybe a swim and a massage. Coffee with an old friend — or some new ones. Plus, she'd had an email from the school, asking all parents to bring their kids in early. She kept quiet about that.

Pupils lined either side of the pathway as Tom and Sarah stepped through the gates. Tom raised his eyebrows. He didn't want any fuss. The headmaster was standing at the main entrance. He waved a greeting, and the staff, behind him, broke into applause.

"Oh, God," Tom groaned.

"I'm sure it'll all settle down soon," said Mary. "Meantime, enjoy it. It's well deserved."

"Come on Sarah," said Tom, glumly. "Please stick to me like glue."

Mary's eyes were filling up. "Enjoy your day, both of you," she called after them through her tears, watched her two amazing kids march towards the entrance. The other kids stamped their feet, clapped and cheered. Tom and Sarah reached the top step, turned and waved. Lots of phones were out, taking photos. The headmaster coughed. Tom turned and met his outstretched hand.

"Thank you, sir," he said. "It's too much, but thank you."

Everyone gradually made their way into the building. Tom and Sarah put their bags in their lockers, ready for assembly. He pulled Sarah out of the stampede, and kissed her cheek. Hands joined, they made their way to the large hall, packed with pupils and parents. Silence fell as the headmaster raised his hands.

"Ladies and gentlemen, welcome back," he roared. "Today is the start of a new year, a new term, and a new chance for us all to learn new things. But before we sing our hymn, I'd like to ask a true hero to take the stage and say a few words. Come on up here, Thomas Drake!"

Tom looked at Sarah and rolled his eyes. "This is all I need," he said.

Standing tall, he walked to the stage, not at all sure what to say. He took a deep breath, smiled at Sarah, and spoke from his heart.

"Thank you all for that wonderful welcome," he said. "But I'm not a hero. I'm just a boy. When that bullet hit me, I thought I was going to die. I've never felt pain like it. It was my dad and the paramedic who were heroes. They saved my life. They gave me a second chance, and I'm going to grab it with both hands — well, once my shoulder is better I will."

A quiet chuckle ran around the room, as Tom tried to think of what to say next. "No, I'm definitely not a hero," he said. "But I *am* lucky. I have amazing parents. I live in a warm home. I eat good food — and I'm loved.

If it wasn't for that, for my parents and my wonderful girlfriend Sarah, I wouldn't be standing here today. They give me strength and courage. They're my heroes.

"Some people aren't so lucky," he went on. "And I guess, more than anything, I've learned that I want to change that. I want to make things better, to make sure there's more good than evil in the world. So here's what I want. I want us all to stand together. To change things for the better. To stand up for what's right. Because we can, and because we care. If we don't do that, what's the point of being here? It's not about one hero looking after everyone else. It's about all of us. Every one of us. Looking after each other."

The hall was silent. Tom blushed a little, wondering if he sounded like a total nerd. But in fact, his audience was simply stunned. Mary, who had secretly stayed behind to film her boy, was almost bursting with pride. "What a boy," she thought. "Our boy. Our boy Tom." She had no doubt that one day this boy would change the world.

As Mary walked back to her car, she felt the ground begin to shake. It was coming from the hall, from the stomping of feet, rapturous applause and chanting of 'Thomas, Thomas, Thomas!' What a great start to the day. She sat in her car, crying and beaming, and shared her video with Jason.

Assembly came to an end. The pupils made their way to class. In the corridor, a new boy nudged into Tom. "Oh, sorry!" he said. "I hope I didn't bash your shoulder? Great speech, Tom. I'm Steven Johnson, just started today. Mind if I tag along with you two?"

Tom looked at Steven Johnson, stared into his black, soulless eyes. A shiver went down his spine as he realised the spirit that had possessed the Eagle was still very much at large. He nodded, and held out his hand. It was holding his bible. *Keep your friends close...* he thought.

"If you're going to fit in here," he said, in a friendly voice, "You'll need one of these. Welcome. To my world." Johnson blazed a stare at Tom, dropped the Bible, turned sharply and walked away. Tom picked up the little book, and tucked it safely back in his bag. The battle had only just begun, but he was ready. He took Sarah by the hand and they went to class.

Epilogue

That evening, Sarah put her diary away and stared out of the window at the clear, dark sky. Millions of stars twinkled down, more than she'd ever seen. She was thinking, peacefully, about her new life. Her guardian angel must surely have waved some kind of celestial magic wand. She drifted back, thinking of her past. She imagined telling Tom the truth. No. He'd never believe her. Just imagine it...

"I had a massive heart attack on my 40th birthday, and woke up in a dazzling white room. There was a woman in a white flowing dress. Her voice was soft and musical. "Hello, Sarah," she said. "There's been a change of plan. I'm sending you back – you've got a job to do."